Love Lamentations

Love Lamentations

A Novel

Rajeev Bector

To my best friend, Stephen. Thank you for your sense of humor, for always being there through thick and thin, and most of all, for your friendship. This book is dedicated to you.

"Grow weary if you will, let me be sad.
Use no more speech now;
Let the silence spread gold hair above us,
Fold on delicate fold."

RICHARD ALDINGTON

Contents

Author's Note

Throughout our lives we are on a quest to know ourselves. As children we readily adopt different personas and identities to determine the best fit. As we mature, and particularly as we experience loss and setbacks, we are ejected into a void of doubt and uncertainty. How do we then recalibrate to develop a narrative that is coherent and meaningful?

Depicting an event, whether real or imagined, is perhaps less consequential than the human emotion and experience undergirding it. But the mere attempt to depict that emotion somehow changes the nature and character of the experience itself. It is always possible to embellish what should be unadorned and genuine, whether through misrepresentation or omission. This idea has been echoed by multiple writers. Ernest Hemingway once remarked that the most essential gift for a good writer is a "built-in, shockproof, shit detector." And Langston Hughes takes his instructor's advice to heart in his poem, "Theme for English B" to "Go home and write / a page tonight. / And let that page come out of you— / Then, it will be true."

And yet, isn't that the nature of language itself, that something is invariably lost as the electrical signals are converted from their conception in the mind to their manifestation on the page or the screen? Words and images may be imperfect approximations of our true emotional states, but it is still the author's responsibility to plumb the depths of the human psyche and to lend a fresh perspective to the familiar and mundane by underscoring our interconnectedness and shared humanity. One must continually strive toward something greater than oneself. As Browning puts it, "A man's reach should exceed his grasp, / Or what's a heaven for?"

Chapter One

I Have Had Enough!

Maya's first pregnancy was largely uneventful. In nine months she had given birth to a healthy baby daughter. Her second pregnancy ended in a stillborn after five months. We didn't name the child, and I only dimly remember the drive to the funeral parlor, the stuffy, dark mahogany interior, signing a few papers, and cutting a check for the cremation. The nameless and faceless funeral director sat me down for the formalities and glumly muttered, "Very sorry for your loss."

When Maya became pregnant for the third time our relationship had already begun to deteriorate. Some people confuse lust with love or use these terms interchangeably, but these were two distinct concepts in my mind. I would return home after working 11 or 12 hours on some days, play with my baby-girl while Maya fixed dinner, then eat, stare into space, or admire the indentations on the living room wall, and then turn in. We had little to say to one another. I had grown up in New York City, on a steady diet of western hegemony, capitalist thought, and particular ideas about the sanctity of the literary canon; Maya had earned a bachelor's degree in history from a university in Punjab, in the Punjabi language. There's something to the bit about reaping what you sow: When I was nine or ten, I would spend my days catching house flies and big black ants, trapping them together in an empty glass bottle, and observing the interaction for hours. And so, the two of us were from two different worlds, united by our ancestry, but with no common frame of reference and no desire to understand one another.

In many ways Maya's pregnancy was an attempt on my part to salvage our marriage and to build a family, but the riptide of kismet had already taken us far from the shore. We were, as it were, not waving, but drowning. In retrospect, I can admit to myself that I was not thinking, just feeling—a feeling that we were being pulled apart by forces too big for us to comprehend. So, I did what I could at that moment, feeling the need to shore up my defenses against this vast monstrosity of an impersonal, indifferent universe, and fathered a son. And yet, how could this child, being a product of adverse circumstances, really compete in this world? Does creation from chaos leave you that much more prepared to face adversity, or disadvantage you against your luckier peers?

Sometime in the first trimester I bought some test strips, even though I knew the damage had been done. There was the usual hand-wringing about finances, care-giving challenges for our first-born while this new egg hatched, and the importance, ever greater now, of aspiring to a less mundane existence; of somehow being able to eschew those twice weekly trips to the grocery stores and the hours spent at the laundromat on weekends, which left me less and less time for pursuing my own oneness.

Chapter Two

The Journey Changes Everything

So I decided to chuck it all. It took three months of emotional turbulence and moral angst to work up the courage to move from thought to deed. First, I wrote to the government to withdraw my petition for Maya's permanent residency. And when in the middle of sending it via courier she called to inquire about why I was still at work, I smugly responded inwardly that I was doing her work, or rather, doing her in! Then, there were itineraries to be built, separate ones, reflecting the divergence of our paths. The planning was meticulous. Every little detail had been attended to: from the plane tickets, to hotel bookings, to my preparations for my own escape. I had it down pat.

I took the train back from work and stared at strangers' faces, and wrestled with the idea for days, then weeks, then months. Often minutes would go by simply standing and staring in the mirror in the bathroom, contemplating the water in my cupped hands, and staring into the abyss.

Throughout the 15-hour flight I drifted in and out of consciousness. It was too much of an effort to try to distract myself, while the wench seated next to me watched her Hindi movies and encouraged me to do the same. After almost three years of marriage she should have known better.

Finally, the plane touched down at Indira Gandhi International

Airport. The drive to the hotel through dusty streets ended with an abrupt halt. The hotel, a fortress, rose contemptuously above the commotion of the city below. Hotel security looked into the taxi and lowered the collapsible metal bollards into the ground to let us proceed. Once at the door, more security checks. The road to freedom led through this maximum-security prison, where I arrived willingly to be free and clear forever. I cannot remember whether it was day or night when we arrived and prefer to remain ignorant of this shadow time of subtle influences. I only remember checking in at the hotel and asking the front desk for two double beds. That night she tossed and moaned and so I invited her to my bed and let her hands roam over my body. She protested that all that was left now was caressing and touching. And so we were left groping, trying to feel with our fingers what our eyes were blind to see.

The next morning, Samster, as my sister used to refer to her friend, called me at the hotel and "reminded" me to pick up her things she wanted to send to my sister. Before I left, we walked a bit in the hotel lobby and on the weedy grounds and she got winded from the effort.

"See?" I said. "Just a walk around the hotel and you are panting. How can you possibly accompany me to the bazaar to see Samster?"

She looked worried. "But I don't want you to go either! What if something happens to you? Lots of things can happen in this city!"

I bit my lip. Indeed! Lots that one cannot possibly imagine! I enticed her with the promise of something tasty from the coffee shop. "I will bring you something nice before I go."

"By the way," she asked, "why is that woman named 'Samster'? That's not an Indian name."

"No, it's not, but it's just two friends teasing each other. She calls Meena 'Meanster,' and so Meena calls her 'Samster.' Her real name is Smriti. Anyway, do you want anything?"

"What? French Fries and a burger?"

"If that's what you want."

"Okay, but hurry back." She reclined on the bed, and I called a cab to take me to the nearby shops. Walking was out of the question through the maze of traffic, construction, noise, and the buzzing and swarming of so many people.

I had already taken the precaution of putting my toiletries and other necessaries in the duffel bag I had brought and deposited this at the front desk; all the easier to make my escape. Little did I know at the time that she and her family would look at the footage from the closed-circuit cameras the next day and see me retrieve my bag and calmly saunter out of the hotel.

I gave her the food and 800 rupees and started off; but how could I leave before our formality of kissing on the lips with closed mouths, as was our custom? I hesitated for a moment near the elevators, thinking maybe I wasn't leaving her enough money.

"Nonsense!" a voice cried inside my head. "Enough with the sappiness and muddled thinking. You have a plane to catch!"

Sometimes there are signs and symbols all around, which in the moment do not appear as such, but only later upon reflection. I had a few such signs of my impending difficulties from the moment I got in the cab. The cabbie was under the impression that I was to be transported to Chandni Chowk, a rather bustling, crowded market a 40-minute drive from the hotel. I told him I had to pick up a friend from the airport first, and so he should go there immediately. During the ride he started to convince me that he was absolutely the best driver and that I must call him as soon as I got out of the airport. And I began to wonder if I would even be allowed to leave the cab unless I agreed to take his phone number and become best buds with him!

Once out of the cab, the sprint to the ticket counter was instantaneous: up the ramp and through the sliding doors of the airport. Next thing I know, a petite young lady with slightly arched eyebrows in her airport uniform is looking me over with bemused curiosity.

First, the obligatory questions:

"Are you traveling alone?"

"Yes."

"How many days did you spend in India?"

"Two." I lied. It was not even 24 hours yet.

"Where are you traveling to?"

"London." This much was true. I had planned on going there when I booked the ticket.

And now, the real meat and potatoes. She gestured at the small duffel bag I was carrying, "Is this your only luggage?"

"Yes. I travel light." Luckily, I had the presence of mind to bring even this much when I started from the hotel.

"Aarti, here is another one with no luggage!"

So that's how it ends! I thought to myself.

But that was just the beginning. During the slow progression of one of many lines leading up to the gate—I think it was the security line—I kept on shuffling her passport and mine from one pocket to another. At first I reasoned that two passports in one pocket might bulge too much and put them in separate pockets, but then second guessed myself. What if I am asked to produce my passport and forget which pocket to reach into? Fishing one out, and then the other, would land me in hot water with an observant official (an oxymoron, I know). And then, during this shuffling, I looked up and saw closed circuit cameras all around me. I like to believe that as this situation was unfolding I was fully conscious of its sheer absurdity and even able to laugh at myself a little bit. But then again, I give myself too much credit sometimes.

Another interminable and lugubrious plane ride! Here I was, with my air-drawn dagger, stabbing my conscience, and gushing with pangs of remorse with each stab. I dared not think on what I had done, yet that's all there was to do until I landed in London.

Chapter Three

A Shakespearean Tragedy

L ondon! What a town! I remember my first trip there, eons ago, sitting next to an exquisitely beautiful British girl, and hearing her remark that it must be so nice to live in New York, and thinking the same about her life in London. And all through the flight I had tried to read *Measure for Measure*, rather conspicuously, to try to impress her; doubtless, it probably had the opposite effect. Still, this first trip was in the summertime, and it was just short of divine. I took in all the touristy sights: Big Ben, Harrods, the Tower of London, London Bridge, a boat tour, The Globe Theatre, double decker buses, and a lush, leafy park in the middle of the city.

But, as with everything, there was a darker side to my sunny sojourn in London. My original plan had been to visit New Delhi and then to Jalandhar to spend a few weeks with my first wife, Anu. As was customary, our whole family had gone to New Delhi, after getting some responses to an ad placed in the local papers there, and then met up with the Bhatias. They had seemed nice, and normal enough, and so we had made plans to set a marriage date. The marriage had largely been a sordid affair: all that travel, then the formalities of the rituals, the special shoes and wardrobes, all the noise and pomp of the wedding band, as it waded slowly through the narrow streets, with onlookers craning their necks and leaning precariously over their balconies. So many people danced on the street, holding up the carriage and forcing me to wait out this foolishness. The crowds, the ceremonies, the singeing heat of the lighting lamps and the noise from the incessant beating of the drums and the caterwauling trumpets and trombones, all of that had taken an immense mental toll on me; and I writhed like a worm, eager to wriggle free. The rented hall itself was rather dilapidated, what with mud floors, substandard toilets with stained stalls, and the rickety little stage they had put together hurriedly for seating Anu and me, while the hired performers danced and sang, in what seemed like an interminable string of events on our wedding night. When it finally ended, everyone was too exhausted to even exhale.

The next day offered no reprieve. There were errands to run, before our return trip to New York, and someone had suggested visiting the Canadian embassy to process Anu's visitor visa so she could come and visit us in two or three months. What a hair-brained idea, but we went along with it anyway! With only two or three days left on the trip, one wanted at least to consummate the marriage! Not so easy to do so, however, when the whole family is shut up together in a three-bedroom rented apartment, the bedroom walls adjoined, and two single beds in our room, with a sentry of a nightstand in the middle. After the first night sleeping apart, my folks put the beds together, and embarrassing as that was, at least it allowed for coitus! I was particularly startled right before the consummation when I heard a sudden "pop!" from her groin. I was no virgin, having been with at least two other women before, but something like this had never happened. My member had the sensation of suffocation and stickiness, and I couldn't help wondering then if that's how Indian women were or if Anu had particularly strong pelvic muscles. It wasn't all serious stuff of course; we played games too. I told her, for instance, that one of my fantasies was seeing her pee. So she indulged me shortly and invited me to the bathroom. She was sitting on the commode, and it sure seemed as if she really were urinating, but I knew the flush had a faulty washer and the water kept leaking into the pot. I called her out on it, and we had a hearty laugh.

In another day or two, it was time to part. We were at the airport, ready to board our flight home. Anu's family had come to bid us farewell. There was the usual commotion of a busy check-in area, what with the fourteen thousand formalities and security checks one had to undergo. She watched me like a cat from behind the glass partition of the terminal, her eyes full of longing. The sadness permeated my being, and it still haunts me when I reflect on those days.

So why did it all fall apart? I know why, but the why doesn't satisfy me and it doesn't assuage the spirit or soothe the soul. There was a third wheel between us, and this interloper has been with me during my formative years and young adult life, shaping my existence. At the time of our wedding I was just a permanent resident in my adopted homeland, and to put it simply, belonged neither here nor there. A few months later, when I made plans to visit Anu in New Delhi and then to travel to Punjab, my immigration status had not changed. Anu's parents, meanwhile, consulted with their relatives and became upset because the marriage had never been registered in an Indian court of law. But we argued that registering the marriage would lengthen the time it would take Anu to join me in America since I could not bring her on a fiancée visa prior to obtaining citizenship. But these technicalities seemed to them evasive maneuvers on my part, and they made clear that once I arrived the marriage would be registered. So, instead of making London just a stopover, I decided it was best to make it the final destination and never continue on the journey to New Delhi. This proved fatal to the marriage and Anu filed for divorce, on the grounds that I was impotent.

A few years later, I chatted up another girl from the suburbs of London on a dating website. We had long, serious, platonic conversations for months on end. She was two years older than me, and sometimes our conversations revolved around how I felt talking (and presumably) wanting to marry someone older than me. She told me about the time she came to America and was shocked that there were no streetlights in the countryside. I told her that in all fairness America is a huge country compared to Britain, and it would be prohibitively expensive to put streetlights along every road in the nation, though certainly not impossible of course. She brought this up because she had traveled to America a few weeks ago to meet a guy somewhere in Wisconsin or in the Midwest, but apparently it hadn't worked out. So we kept conversing for more than six months, and then I decided to go and meet her in person.

Everything seemed to be fine. Only she kept mentioning that I was coming around the Christmas holidays and most of London would be closed at that time. I told her not to worry, that we will be together, and the world around us will just sort of dissolve away, like in that poem, "Ah love, let us be true / to one another! for the world which seems / to lie before us like a land of dreams . . . ." And lo and behold! I landed in London and her whole family, minus her father (not sure whether he was even still alive, and if not, I don't blame him), came to the airport to drop me off at my hotel. Her brother drove the car, with her mother in the passenger seat in the front and us lovebirds in the back. She made minimal conversation and looked out her window. I chalked it up to diffidence, modesty, and generosity (so that I may take in the views of London at night.) Finally, after zigzagging across the city we reached the Ibis Hotel where I was lodging. Her brother had been running red lights trying to find the right Ibis among the countless others in that part of town, and her mother had been muttering something about hundred pounds under her breath every time her boy drove too fast around the ubiquitous red-light cameras.

The next morning I skipped the hotel breakfast (despite the fact that the English are renowned for their cuisine) and went straight to one of those red phone booths.

"Hello, may I speak to Rashmi please?"

"Who is this?"

"This is Ajay. Remember, you picked me up at the airport yesterday?"

"Hold on."

A long silence.

"Hi, yes. Ajay?"

"Good morning Rashmi, How are you?"

"Fine."

"Do you want to meet up in the city?"

"No, I can't. Why don't you meet me at my home? Just come to Harrow and call me once you get there."

I thought it a bit strange but relented.

"All right. And then call you from a phone booth?"

"Yes."

She hung up.

The day was raw and cold. I blew on my cracked, red knuckles, lest they turn blue from the cold, and boarded the train, ready for an adventure.

Harrow. Upon alighting I saw a sign that said, "Courage" painted in big bold letters on the side of a building. Two smokestacks were belching out black soot.

Another call. Another moment of silence as I held the line. First the mother spoke, saying Rashmi could not talk, but I insisted.

"Rashmi, I am here. Where is your house?"

"I am sorry, but I've changed my mind."

"What do you mean?"

"Changed my mind, that's all."

"Is this a joke?"

"I went to America a few months ago. You must remember that?"

"I do."

"So there you are. I went all the way there with my brother, and this American man rejected me. I am just returning the favor."

"Are you crazy?" I blurted.

"No, quite sane. You are the crazy one, coming all the way out here to see me. Goodbye."

I must have stood holding the receiver for a good minute or two, agape at the hand dealt me.

There was nothing to do but return to London. It was late afternoon on Christmas Eve as I finally got back to the city. The hotel was a bit far for a walk, so I thought I might take a bus, but this being a Christian country, there were no buses running on this day and at this hour. Plodding along, an old woman wished me, "Happy Christmas," and that made me fume. Pangs of hunger had now started, and I realized I had not eaten all day. Most restaurants seemed closed. A freezing rain was falling, and I scurried along the narrow alleyways.

Chapter Four

Trash Talk

But I digress! London was a washout, not because of the precipitation, and not because of the events that precipitated my visit, but in the more vernacular sense of being "washed up" as my students taught me some years ago when I was teaching high school English.

When I reached the hotel room I was astounded. Such profound silence! After hearing the roar of the plane's engines for more than eight hours and listening to the interminable "music of the spheres" emanating from my beloved's lips for the past two plus years of our marriage, the silence was deliciously divine. I felt my intelligence and curiosity, and indeed my very soul, rebound after just a day of solitude. As the hours went by, I began to cherish my newfound freedom, not just physical, but intellectual and emotional and spiritual. Oh, to be able to think thoughts I wanted to think for as long as I desired! To be free to debate, question, and discuss whatever I wanted with myself! I was here for the next two days. The next morning, I bought a sweatshirt from a souvenir shop after much hand-wringing and exchange rate lookups. A misty rain was falling, and I darted into a sketchy cul-de-sac and found an Indian restaurant to escape the cold. The papadum was delicious and the place had a whorehouse feel to it. Long strings of beads hung everywhere, and nubile young women served the customers. It was as if I had been transported back to the lonely days of my younger years.

Early in the evening, Meena called me to ask whether I still had the "things I should not have" upon my person.

"Yes, I have it. Why?"

"Destroy them then. Cut them up in little pieces and throw them away. Why do you want to hang on to it now?"

"Where will I get the scissors from?" I asked, innocently.

"Don't be an idiot. Buy them, get them from the hotel, cut them up and throw them down the toilet."

The project had a special, mystical significance to it, and I would perform it with great gusto.

I cut up all her documents into thin little strips and then crosscut them. Then I mixed it all together, as if preparing a party mix, and wrapped it up in a sheet of paper. But the party mix was for a big party, and I was just a party of one, so some of it had to go right away. Now was the time for a test. A test of the London septic system. After ten or twelve flushes I stopped, for now my load was much more manageable. Besides, it was time for dinner and being a vegetarian who was in no mood for fish and chips, the obvious choice was Chinese food.

The restaurant was classy enough, and the restrooms afforded privacy for another bout of flushing. For such an old septic system, it surpassed all my expectations! With nothing but a few more pieces left now, I took to the road, strewing some along my way surreptitiously after looking left and right. The rest I deposited in a trash can by a bus stop, and fancied that I was rid of it forever, and by extension, of her as well.

This being London and the locals having such a reputation for gregariousness, I decided to socialize with some newfound friends: pain, misery, guilt, and a deep and abiding sadness. I even managed to smuggle all of them on my flight back to New York!

Chapter Five

April is the Cruellest Month

N ew York, New York! What a wonderful town! Hold your head up, even when the chips are down. "I am Lazarus, come from the dead, come back to tell you all, I shall tell you all." No, it wasn't quite like that, but close. I was a zombie for months afterward but could give no voice to my woe. The surroundings were familiar, the people were the same, but a haze had taken root in my brain, and I had no appetite for life anymore.

First, my parents told me stories that could not be told over the phone. Evidently, Maya's father, brother, and uncle had arrived, finally, after I left the hotel. They had made phone calls all over the globe, used the business center, ordered room service several times, examined video footage of my departure, and filed a criminal complaint, charging me with abandonment and fraud. All told, the hotel bill for two or three days amounted to more than a thousand dollars. They had called my parents to ask about their level of involvement and complicity in my doings. Maya had gotten on the line and challenged my parents to keep Iris from her, our only child at the time, for much longer. The whole family had been threatened with legal action and dire consequences. Of course, my parents and sister denied all knowledge of my actions, there being no other real choice. Jaura, this bloated, amorphous amoeba, resembling Jabba the Hutt, had bubbled out of somewhere and started with his threats. Jaura was Maya's uncle, or more precisely her mother's younger brother. He had harangued my parents so much in India, pressuring them to consider and then reconsider Maya after I had initially rejected her for lacking a personality, that I took pity on them, and on myself, and agreed to sponsor her on a fiancée visa.

Our place was a war-room for days, with long, protracted strategy sessions on how to respond to this woman who was raising hell from thousands of miles away and hurling accusations left and right. Suddenly, my business had become everyone's business. My sister drew up a comprehensive list of atrocities committed by Maya and it amazed me to see how all the little details added up. We were living with a psychopath all these years! In retrospect, I had known all along that this was the case even before our wedding. Many times she would simply leave in the middle of a conversation if things did not go her way or threaten to commit suicide and even try to follow up on her threat. I chalked it up to immaturity and paid no mind to it at the time, but one has to pay sooner or later, in one form or another.

I was shuttling back and forth between the apartment I still maintained and my parents' place. It was hard to give up on my own place, where I could invite anyone over that I suspected of possessing a central nervous system, (though, in reality, hardly any girl ever accepted my invites), and where I could roam around naked, sleep naked, eat naked, and so on. But my little girl was with my parents and seeing her for only an hour did not do her justice. One day she looked wistfully after me and her visage saddened after I waved her goodbye to return to my apartment. After that I decided to act a bit more responsibly. After all, I was not a single guy anymore. I had my parents and my child to care for. Or, more accurately, my parents had me and their grandchild to care for.

My dad had filed his retirement papers and was urging my mom to do the same. With a toddler less than two years of age at home, it was a bit much for him to manage all by himself. We began taking days off from work to provide childcare. One warm April day, having taken the day off from work, I was watching TV with Iris and looking out at the overcast sky; I began to think of my unborn child and what had become of him. I knew he was still unborn, and his mother was opposed to the idea of terminating her pregnancy. And yet, it seemed incredible that he would now be born in India, and perhaps never be able to come to America, where he rightfully belonged.

My luck changed for the worse the next day. We were all gathered around the dinner table when the wench called my dad. Dad talked to her for a minute then hung up, dumbfounded. She had called from a payphone right outside our apartment building, asking to be let in. Driving to the building with dad, I knew then that my life was over. All the years of sweat and toil, of back-breaking, eye-glazing, neck-twisting, unpleasant work, all for naught.

Chapter Six

Aftermath

It was a lovely Spring evening. The crickets had started their nocturnal chirping, and it was too early for fireflies. There was a light breeze and some high clouds. I had taken my shopping cart with me to bring back my stuff from the apartment. The thought of staying with the wench was unbearable. How in the world could she have clawed her way back?

She smiled a smug smile when she saw me. There was more than an inordinate amount of satisfaction and vengeance on her visage. She started going toward the back entrance of the building and stopped short.

"Oh, the bags are out by the front."

I kept mum. Typical absentmindedness on her part. Heck, she had left the rice cooker half full of rice with yogurt mixed in it just lying on the counter all those days we were in India. Only a day or two after my return had I noticed it, and by that time it had grown moldy. The apartment seemed like it had not been cleaned for months, with dust bunnies everywhere and mold and mildew in the shower. I had to straighten everything out, put things and people (like Maya) back in their place, clean out the microwave, organize the shoe closet, vacuum, mop – the works! The miserable wench.

Two large bags and a surly-looking fellow greeted us in the

building lobby. The man gave me a good once-over and left, after looking sympathetically at Maya. I rushed upstairs, telling her to wait in the lobby, mumbling that I needed to get something from the apartment. As soon as I entered, I began packing frantically, and more like dumping everything in sight into the shopping cart. Hardly five minutes into this frenzy I heard a loud banging on the front door. She had left her bags downstairs and had come charging up, demanding to be let in. Another mad, frantic rush. Grab what you can. Tear up all the garbage and salvage what you will. I got most things, but the computer and monitor remained. Fortunately, I had changed the password already so she could not log on.

I did not sleep that night. Some lines of a poem kept reverberating in my head:

> O plunge your hands in water,
> Plunge them in up to the wrist;
> Stare, stare in the basin
> And wonder what you've missed.

I looked deep into my eyes in the mirror and stared and stared. The darkness in my soul was palpable, oppressive, suffocating. I had gazed long enough into the abyss, and indeed the abyss was gazing back at me.

My sister and I traveled back to the apartment the next afternoon. Maya was in the shower and only later realized that we had opened the door and marched in. I packed up my remaining necessaries and took the computer and whatever else I could stuff in my shopping cart. As we were leaving, she came out of the bathroom, looking surprised and angry. Then she ran into her room, closed the door, and started making a phone call to someone. When we were down the lobby, she came running and asked to speak to me for a few minutes. My sister took my personal effects to the car and I stayed behind.

I stared at her for some time, scrutinizing her face.

"So, why did you come back?

"To settle our home and keep our family together, of course."

"Oh yes, of course."

A tense silence. The kind where each party is aware of the other's mendacity.

"You must be so shocked to see me here!" she blurted.

"More like disappointed that you did not show up as scheduled."

"Oh, please!"

"So, what do you want from me?"

"When are you coming back and bringing our daughter?"

"You must be mad!"

She glared at me. I turned and walked away. What more was there to say? Then, thinking of something:

"By the way, my phone number has changed. I can tell you if you need it."

"I don't have a pen or paper."

"Then memorize it." I rattled off the digits. She seemed to be internalizing the numbers.

"The kid is sick. We are taking her to the doctor. You can come if you like."

"Maybe later."

"Fine then."

Back in the car, my dear sister was waiting for me to start her grilling: "What did you two talk about? Is that all you talked about in the half-hour you were with her? Did you say anything else? What did she say?"

Chapter Seven

The Ache of Marriage

Anyone contemplating marriage should consult with those who are divorced. It is a nether world, all its own! And it certainly doesn't help if your partner is obtuse and illiterate, from a no-name village in the middle of nowhere, yet thinks they are royalty. I can still see the exasperation in my attorney's face as he tried to explain why I must be made a financial martyr by flailing his arms and blurting, "This is who you married!" Married someone who didn't have a cent to her name, no people skills, no conversational skills, no real education beyond a degree on paper. I can go on and on, but what's the use? There was desperation in me too that drove me to it, and maybe a cavalier sense of invincibility, tempered with deference to my parents' wishes. And there was a sense of practicality too: did I really want to continue to associate with loose and vulgar women my whole life? I had already been to brothels twice and was an established serial dater. How much longer could this go on?

Now the real work began. After the day's work, my sister and I, and sometimes the whole family, would make the rounds to lawyers' offices. The first guy we went to see was so benevolent and relaxed, as opposed to the high anxiety and high-tension state we were in, that I thought we were at the offices of the Godfather. All he needed was a raspy voice and a few gestures with his hands to make the transformation complete. He talked incessantly about how the two kids should not be separated and how the courts would never consider separating them. All I remember of him ultimately, aside from the princely sum for his retainer, was the image of a genial white guy speaking softly behind closed office doors, among his plush furnishings and polished mahogany furniture. The second lawyer was a tall, white, middle-aged man. Arranged among his papers and other paraphernalia were framed photographs of his three kids. He seemed to be more of an attorney-at-interruption than an attorney-at-law. After every sentence, or sometimes in mid-sentence, I would be cut-off so his eminence might jot things down, take notes on his computer, or quite simply think. I appreciated him for being so thorough and thoughtful but resented him for making me defend myself.

"Why do you want a divorce?" he asked.

"Well, for a lot of reasons. For instance, my wife can't take care of the kid—"

"Can't take care? What do you mean, can't take care?"

"I mean, she dropped her in the tub one day, then she dropped her from the bed another day. Just can't take care--"

"I have three kids, and they are jumping up and down like monkeys all day, banging their heads, running around etc. So, things like this are part of normal life."

"Well, she has anger management issues and things like that. I really don't want to go into it."

"Listen," he said. "Custody is an uphill battle. And when you are halfway through it you will stop and wonder why you are fighting it in the first place."

"Yes, I understand," I said obligingly.

But it was really Maureen, the third attorney, who allayed our concerns while simultaneously heightening them. She asked calmly about the situation and listened attentively. And when it came to dispensing advice she applied the personal touch.

"Well, this is what I would do if it were a member of my own family: she might file for custody soon, so don't delay. Go to the courthouse as soon as you can and file for your daughter. I can send you the form and the paperwork to make it easier."

My parents and I left the office feeling valued and respected, like we had finally been heard, but also with a new sense of urgency.

Chapter Eight

Tell All the Truth But Tell it Slant

Sometimes recalling what came to pass and when is akin to peering through a thick curtain of rain at dusk: the sky bleeds into the earth and coalesces into a gray and nebulous affair. Easy to say after the fact, of course. In the moment every twitch is a life-or-death decision. So, I took a day off from the most important job in the world of being an Assistant Principal in a failing school that was being phased out anyway and went to court. I remember driving there through the downpour, and standing breathless in the pendant air, watching the clerk look disapprovingly over my papers.

"Is this the original?" she asked.

"Yes, of course," I lied. Being new to all this, I had just carelessly ripped off the original and put it through the shredder. Who wants to carry hundreds of copies of this stuff anyway? Kind of reminds me of the time when I went before the immigration judge, and he asked me to raise my right hand and swear to tell the truth. I raised my left, standing very erect and forthrightly, and proceeded to give my account. My dad just stared at me then, being in the witness stand himself, but I never heard the end of it for the rest of my life. "Oh, he just raised his left hand and proceeded to answer the judge. My God!" My dad would exclaim to anyone and everyone who would give him an audience.

We all have such high expectations and dreams for our children. Somehow, they are special. They were made in God's image, while the rest are just unremarkable functionaries whose sole function is to help our progeny succeed, and to make them shine. That was my hope for my child too (it was just my one child when I decided to part ways), but more than that it was the visceral fear that if I didn't take the initiative, this woman would eventually leave me anyway and go marry a taxi driver or a construction worker; and then that man would abuse my daughter, maybe even making the mother complicit in the crime, since she depended on him financially. Most of all it was the nightly protestations and cries from the child who would, presumably after sleeping all day, look for any excuse to avoid bedtime until late at night, and her cries penetrated my drowsy consciousness through two closed doors. I promised my daughter then, silently, that I would do right by her. I fancied saying to her, "Don't worry, sweetheart, I am working on it. I will do something for you." And why not? As I began to spend more time with Iris I became more emotionally invested in her. For the first few days of her life she inhabited her own world. On one occasion, for instance, she fixed her gaze at the ceiling and laughed audibly, for no apparent reason; and so, in keeping with the dogma of our Indian traditions and mental models, we ascribed that to a memory of her former life, now surfacing into her consciousness. As time went on, however, and she became more self-aware, she would look at the trees and notice the twittering of the sparrows during our evening jaunts in the summers. Mother remembered fondly how Iris arrived at her grandparents' home, after months sometimes, and would still be able to recall the exact location of each lamp in the living room and pointed to the same. When she started school, I began to appreciate her math acumen and burgeoning verbal and inferential skills, as evidenced by her recognition and use of puns and double-entendres. And so I started doing my part by explaining to her the workings of this world, insofar as I was able.

∞ ∞ ∞

The clerk smirked. "No, sir, this is not the original. You have to bring me the original."

"But it is notarized, and I think it is the original."

"No, no, no!" She shook her head slowly with closed eyes. Then she looked intently at me. "See here, this is a court of law. We have to follow the procedure here. Please come back with the original."

So there I was, driving back, running to the bank again, getting the thing notarized and submitting it to the court just in time before it closed for the day. And lucky too! That was a Friday, and on Monday madam herself went to court to file custody for the child, and along with it a writ of habeas corpus. When I heard about it, it simply didn't register at first. I had only seen that word in an impersonal context in a textbook somewhere in college. It just didn't seem that it could ever be applied to my child. Fortunately enough, her actions were moot since I had filed for custody first. The next few months were hazy at best. I don't know by what miracle I managed to hold down a job, engage in spirited and never-ending discussions with my parents, find time for visiting lawyers' offices and make court appearances. Punctuated with all of this were almost daily phone calls from Jaura. He was so emotionally invested in this case, alternately threatening and calmly explaining his views, one would think it was his own affair. And then the other associates of the wench started crawling out of the woodwork: a woman who was supposedly on the President's advisory council on race relations, a jeweler's wife who was sympathetic of Maya and eager to champion her cause, some folks from the domestic violence arena, a "self-made" elderly millionaire, who liked to believe he was the de-facto keeper of the Indian diaspora in Jackson Heights, a businessman who had made his name by getting in early on the cellphone craze back in the day when I was just a teenager, and a TV anchor for an Indian-American network. What a circus!

Between court dates and work and family obligations there was the real-life soap opera of visiting Indian restaurants and spending an evening with these actors, to try and reach a resolution if possible. And so one evening I found myself sitting across the table from Ravinder, the businessman.

"So, Ajay, tell me guy, Maya says you went to India to settle some property dispute and sold some property in India. Is that true?"

"No, I don't have any property in India. I told you, I went to drop her off with her parents since her mother has hernia and needs some help moving about the house. And besides, am I really going to go there and sell off property in a few hours? It's absurd. I don't have any properties in India. I went for her, I told you."

"Very strange. Someone's not telling the truth, for sure."

"Okay, detective. I know I don't have to prove anything to you, and I really don't care what you think."

"Then, why are you here?"

Fortunately, I had done my homework. "You really want to know? How much time do you have?"

Ravinder raised his brows, then looked quizzically at me, as I smiled slyly.

"Here," I said, and slammed the statement I had prepared for the court on the table. "This is my statement to the court. You can read it if you want."

He picked it up and started reading.

As is customary in Indian culture, our marriage was arranged when I visited India in February 20--. I obtained a fiancée visa for Maya upon my May 9, 20-- application. Maya was scheduled to arrive in NY on June 9, 20-- on the basis of that visa. The same day that Maya was to arrive in NY, Maya's brother called me from India claiming that Maya had never boarded the flight, and there was no need for an airport pick-up. He offered no further details or explanation. I was blindsided. I had bought a cell phone for Maya prior to her arrival, set up accommodations for her, and was getting ready to go to the airport to pick her up when I received this call.

Maya finally contacted me after about a month. This is when

I learned that she had arrived as scheduled that day but had left for Texas immediately with her relatives and had lied to me and my family. Maya claimed that she had gotten cold feet before boarding her flight and had arranged for her relatives to pick her up from Texas. She suggested that the marriage should be held in Texas since her cousin was there. I explained to Maya that this was impractical for a variety of reasons, especially since all of our family friends were based in New York and New Jersey, and it would cause them undue hardship to visit Texas for the wedding. Maya refused to listen and called off the wedding. Consequently, after learning of this deception, I wrote to immigration authorities that Maya sought to commit immigration fraud.

Starting October 20-- and continuing until late December 20--, Maya began calling my family regularly to apologize for her behavior and to ask for forgiveness. She admitted that she and her family wanted her to actually marry someone else, but she had learned that, per US law, the fiancée visa I got for her could not be used for this purpose. She sounded distraught, claimed she was being abused by her family members who had taken her from Texas to California to marry another man, and pleaded with my sister, Meena, to save her from these alleged circumstances. I was skeptical and frankly did not want to marry her or have any relationship with her based on this course of events. Maya and certain family members of hers had already proven to be quite untrustworthy.

My family discussed it, and while it was uncertain that we would marry, based upon Maya's claims of coercion and abuse by her cousin, our family decided to shelter her. As a result, my father and sister took a flight to California to rescue Maya, paid for her flight, and brought her to New York on January 15, 20-- as a humanitarian gesture. My parents' home, in which I also resided, was opened to Maya, as she had nowhere else to go at that time.

Maya lived with me and my family for six months. Our culture and beliefs do not permit premarital sex. Maya and I began to become emotionally closer over the months she stayed in our home, and I began to pity Maya. We took a trip together to California in April 20-- and once there she seduced me and we had premarital sex. This became known to my family, and based on conservative family values, they insisted that I marry Maya as originally arranged. We then married in July 20--.

We lived in one room at my parents' home in Floral Park after our marriage, until we moved out to New Jersey in late December 20--. While we lived with my parents and sister, Maya was treated very kindly. My family was able to get her a part-time job at a T-Mobile wireless store and we provided food, shelter, clothing and other discretionary needs for her. I paid handsomely to immigration lawyers to correct Maya's status, as we had not married within the 90 days as required. I paid for various medical needs and tests. I enrolled her in classes to learn English at Queens College and enrolled her in Graduate Equivalency Diploma courses offered by the city of New York.

One of our neighbors, Shelly Smith, often saw and socialized with our family and Maya while we lived across the street from her. Ms. Smith always said that we were "exceedingly kind and considerate toward Maya. Even before Maya's marriage we would take her shopping, to the movies, or to attend cultural and religious events among their circle of friends and acquaintances."

However, despite these efforts by me and my family, Maya obviously had no intention to stay in this marriage and was only perpetuating the same until she could obtain permanent residency status. Maya urged and pressured me to move out from my parents' home, where we had rented one room, with shared kitchen and bathroom facilities. A joint residence of our own would have assisted in her bid for permanent residence. Our daughter, Iris, was born in July 20--. Soon thereafter, Maya complained of being in a "golden cage," unable to go anywhere or do whatever she wanted when she wanted. When Iris was just a few days old, Maya left the newborn unattended while our child was nursing and left the house for the entire day without informing anyone. I drove around the neighborhood showing pictures of Maya frantically, when almost twelve hours later, Maya called me and threatened to commit suicide. She was very unstable.

With great difficulty, I dissuaded Maya from taking any rash action and went to pick her up. I was alarmed and distressed by Maya's suicidal ideation and brought her for treatment and assessment by her primary care physician, Dr. Samantha Rajan. Dr. Rajan recommended a full psychiatric evaluation citing "anger management issues," and provided a referral for the same. Maya did not take those recommendations. Maya again made suicidal threats and started to starve herself in December by refusing food. She continued to pressure me to move out of my parents' home.

Consequently, in an act of desperation, I agreed to move, and we relocated to a small, one-bedroom apartment in Irvington, New Jersey. While this apartment was very far from my workplace and greatly inconvenienced me, I decided to rent it as I could not find anything more economical. While residing in New Jersey, I assisted in Maya's petition for Permanent Resident status.

In early January 20-- we moved back to a Queens apartment to be closer to my family and job. Around March of that year, when Maya was in the early stages of pregnancy, she explained to me that her mother in India had called to implore her to come and assist her, since her mother had developed severe sciatica, had very little mobility, and needed significant assistance. Maya urged me to accompany her. I agreed but made it clear that due to my work schedule I would drop her off with her parents in India, then travel to London for two days, before returning to New York. Maya wanted our daughter Iris to remain in New York with my parents and sister, as they had frequently provided childcare for Iris since she was born, and as Maya was unable to care properly for Iris due to her pregnancy.

I made arrangements for our travel together to India in March 20-- by making reservations to leave in early April 20--. As we finalized the separate dates upon which we would travel back to New York, separate return itineraries were made. My sole purpose for accompanying Maya to India was to drop Maya safely off to her parents. We were to arrive in New Delhi on April 6th 20--, and I was to fly to London the next day on April 7, 20-- and back to New York on April 10, 20--. Maya was to return on April 17th. We arrived in India and checked into our hotel. Maya's family members were to arrive the next day after their journey from Punjab to retrieve her. Her family arrived as scheduled, but I did not check out as they were staying an additional night to rest from their journey from Punjab, and I left my American Express credit card to guarantee all payments. I left to catch my flight on April 7 to London as scheduled.

When I left, Maya had her itinerary, flight information, travel documents, permanent resident card, passport, and belongings. After sightseeing in London, I returned to New York, expecting Maya to also return as planned. When I returned to New York, I was shocked to discover that the hotel bill in India had amounted to 77,654 rupees. Maya and her family had ordered room service multiple times, used the business center, made international calls, and racked up other charges in their short time at the hotel. Had I intended to abandon Maya, I would not have facilitated these expenses to be paid by me, nor checked into a five-star property. Also, after my return, I was baffled to hear through my family that Maya was alleging I stole all her travel documents and surreptitiously abandoned her. She painted my family and me as horrendous abusers.

I was able to contact Maya soon thereafter. I recited to her where she had her documents before I left, and demanded to know why she had made these false and ridiculous allegations. Maya simply continued to level accusations against me. I again asked her to explain how her accusations made any sense given that I had lodged her in such a high-end hotel, forwarded her the airline ticket, reminded her of her flight, and made such efforts to have her return to New York. She made no response. I told her that if she truly did not have her documents, then she should file a police report for the lost passport and contact the American embassy for assistance. Maya had previously established a penchant for making false abuse allegations to get her way. She had largely fabricated the allegations she made against her own cousin and family members, which prompted us to "save" her and transport her to New York from California long prior to our actual marriage. During our marriage, she made some complaints about living with my family, pressured me to get our own apartment, but never made any allegations to me that my mother, my sister, or my father was ever cruel to her in any way.

Although she had been well aware of her return flight plans, I still forwarded Maya a copy by email of her return flight reservation on April 15th. She did not contact me for an extended period of time, did not return my calls, and did not keep me updated with what was going on in India. Mostly, I received harassing phone calls at all hours of the day from her relatives concerning her sudden claims of abuse, and in frustration I changed my phone number. Later, I learned that she had gone to the embassy and filed a report, as I had recommended. Ultimately, she returned to New York without warning, keeping all details of her new itinerary secret from me, and arriving several days after her scheduled return.

Maya called my father on April 29th, twelve days after her regularly scheduled return to New York, wanting to be let into our apartment. She was immediately afforded access. I had moved some of my essential belongings back to my parents' house as it was difficult for me to coordinate care for our daughter Iris, and the best plan was to return to their home. When she returned, I told her I would move back to the apartment and that we might be able to salvage our marriage if she would stop making false and wild allegations. I also informed her that she needed to take our marriage more seriously and responsibly for us to continue to remain married.

The next morning I returned to the apartment. Our daughter was sick and needed a doctor. I informed Maya of the situation, gave her my new cell phone number, and again indicated I would be moving back in within a day or two at the most. She was acting very strange, seemed irate, and ready to instigate something. I left and took our child to the doctor. Around 4:00-5:00 pm, Maya called me and flatly informed me she was leaving me, leaving the door to the apartment unlocked, and the keys in the kitchen drawer. When I returned, I also found she had left her wedding ring on the nightstand. She never returned. She left no address. She abandoned me and our daughter while pregnant with our son.

Soon thereafter, around May 21st of that year, Maya commenced family offense petitions against my mother, my sister and me, in order to continue her master immigration plan allegations of abuse and abandonment. Finally, after carefully considering Maya's actions, her baseless accusations, her lies to me and my family, and the fact that she abused Iris and abandoned me and later our child, not once but four times (after arriving in NY on her fiancée visa, after running away from home when Iris was just an infant, after abandoning Iris by not returning from India on time, and after abandoning her marital home in NY), after all these considerations I realized that for sure our marriage was over and I commenced this action for divorce on May 29th.

In November 20-- Maya gave birth to our son, Kash. This event, which should have been cause for joy and happiness, and indeed jubilation, was instead a sad occasion for our family. Maya did not inform my family or me when or where the child was born, or the sex of the child. She even named the child Ayman Singh, without consulting with me, and using her maiden surname of Singh for the child, when in fact we were married at the time of the child's birth.

As he read, I noticed that everyone was stuffing their mouths and having a jolly old time, and as it seemed to me, all at my expense. One of the self-important dudes there even dropped a samosa into my plate to encourage me to eat, but rage and appetite do not mix well, and hungry as I was, I refused to touch it.

After what seemed like an eternity, Ravinder put the papers down. His visage bore a bewildered expression, and his eyes narrowed. "Well, it's quite a story, isn't it? Is any of it true?"

I was too repulsed to respond.

As the days went by, I came to the realization that I never belonged anywhere. As a boy, I remember playing with insects and reading for hours on end. I always had just one or two friends in whom I confided, and whose company I could abide. And as I grew, this desire for solitude and meditative calm led me to choose a vocation which back then was universally acknowledged to be of a solitary nature. I looked within and discovered that my ideal life would entail reciting poetry and playing chess, and so I went into teaching. The hours were reasonable, and the work was to be done independently when out of the classroom, and to have time in the summers for travelling to tournaments. And yet, this self-knowledge brought neither peace nor contentment. With each passing year I became acutely and painfully aware that the world saw me as a misfit, a loner, an outcast, and that secretly they understood. They saw how naturally averse I was to associations, friendships, and to the company of others. I needn't have said anything as indeed I never did: my face betrayed my antipathy and indifference toward humanity. This being the real world, there were consequences: mostly loneliness. I felt the loneliest in college. Having chosen to study English, sometimes I was the only man among a dozen attractive and shapely young women. This precluded me from meeting and making friends with my male peers, and was not such a godsend as it might have been for a more gregarious and personable individual. Strange as it may sound, the few girls I met either through my own efforts or through dumb luck, I could not impress, having never learned how. The ones who expressed interest in me I could not quite comprehend, until much later after they had given up on me and moved on.

We are all born alone, die alone, so why can't we be alone during our time here? My intelligence had begun to rise substantially after the mindless chatter of this woman had stopped in my ears, so maybe it was a good thing after all. My girl would scream out of boredom, hunger and God knows what else late at night as I covered my ears and tried to catch some sleep, so wasn't it good for her to be rid of that monstrosity of a mother and be raised by loving and caring grandparents who could watch her all the time and indulge their granddaughter? Who knows!

In the days and weeks that followed, there was more fallout and a reckoning as Maya learned I had called her a whore during this meeting, insinuated promiscuity and infidelity on her part, and disowned my own son. The swirl of conjecture and speculation was enough to induce vertigo, with all the angles and possibilities: will I have to pay for the kid in her care now even if I disowned him? Will the shelter officials come after me and demand payment for all the months they had put up Maya and her boy? Will I have to pay for her lawyer and her maintenance? Will it be a long, contested, messy divorce with people being put on the stand? The more people I spoke with, the more of a headache it became. Maya's relatives from India were still calling and bothering my parents. And a new deal-making was afoot to somehow pay off this monstrosity and at least rescue my little girl.

Chapter Nine

Baby, Give it Up!

My dad laid out in minute detail the amount of money I would lose, calculating down to the dollar the share of my pension Maya was entitled to, the likely expenses for the attorneys, the ramifications of equitable distribution, the myriad payments going forward: child support, child care, spousal support and many other egregious legal terms I had hoped never to hear. Talks now began on how to negotiate with someone bent solely on revenge, how to safeguard the toddler in our care, and minimize the financial fallout from the third child. Everyone had their own agenda. My mother was all in for showing up this woman who had plundered our lives through gossip and public shaming, the only trouble with that idea being that Maya was more adept at exploiting the emotions of others and conscripting them to sympathize with her. My sister, in the meantime, urged me to go to the media and make my case through an impassioned appeal to the masses and to buy up all manner of things: furniture, technology, new bedding etc., with the idea that I better spend the money before it was taken away from me.

Little did we know the machinations of our adversary, who had been making the rounds to lawyers' offices and getting in her own preparations. When we made the next requisite court appearance she stood at a distance sizing us up, then made a tentative move and sat across from us.

"I want to discuss something with you, if I can," Maya began.

"We are all ears," I said, with my dad looking on.

"I want to give you custody of Iris!"

I was not amused. "Why would you do that?"

"It's fair. You drop the case for the boy, and I will do the same for Iris."

I could hardly believe my ears. After two years of wrangling and back and forth and all these negotiations, the goal seemed within grasp. I had never wanted any responsibility for the boy to begin with, knowing I could not really care for him. But at the same time I did not really want to have to pay for him all my life either. Being that I was always more motivated by the fear of failure than the prospect of success, I decided to go for it.

"Okay, I will ask my lawyer to draw up an agreement and send it to your lawyer."

Even as I said this I knew it was not true. My lawyer was not worth two licks of work, and I would have to do this all by myself. Her lawyer did not even want to see her too many times out of fear that he would not be compensated for his time and trouble, so for him taking any interest in this was out of the question. All the better for me, I thought; or so it seemed at the time in the absence of any legal advice.

Chapter Ten

Bildungsroman

Our lives begin so innocently, lyrically, so full of promise and beauty. If only they remained so! When I was fourteen, there seemed to be little distinction between my mental state and a stag's during mating season. I would often feel quite audacious and uninhibited even as my father napped across from me in the afternoons in our first tiny apartment in New York. He must have known, or at least suspected, that something was going on. Once I thought he slept a little too lightly with eyes partly open but went ahead anyway with what I had to do. He saw me moving my arm vigorously and asked directly what I was doing. I feigned ignorance and assured him it was nothing but a persistent itch, which was true in a sense, I suppose!

Having visited America twice, my father decided to retire from the Indian Air Force after twenty-two years of service and move to, in his mind, the land of opportunity. Opportunity for better economic prospects, for a fighting chance for his children, away from the madding competition of the East, and an opportunity to reinvent himself, as opposed to the planned obsolescence that awaited him after full retirement, with grown men playing cards in the early morning hours outside their homes, or watching the grass grow in the relentless heat of Delhi summers.

We arrived one fine June afternoon with nothing but the

clothes on our backs and a few small pots and pans hidden in our luggage, hoping they would not be discovered by officials. Yes, pots and pans, not drugs. How the world has changed! After spending a few days with one of dad's acquaintances, we moved into our own apartment, one of many in a housing project, with dimly lit hallways and fish smells and urine pooled in the corners of elevators and stairways, and with a breathtaking view of the glimmering New York skyline. The first few nights we slept on the bare floor, with towels rolled up as pillows. With little more than a few dollars in his pocket, and having borrowed from friends to pay the rent, dad would rise early to wait at the bus stop in the black and blue cold of the winter mornings, and work in the basement of a dusty warehouse, which subsequently gave him asthma and a persistent cough. After that he did whatever came his way: delivering pizza, driving taxicabs, working in a school for the disabled, while mom sewed belts, washed dishes in a restaurant, and walked two miles to work at a retail store. At one time they both worked in a school for half the day, then rushed off to work at a bank, regularly arriving past midnight, in a neighborhood prone to gun violence and muggings, and were victimized by such crimes on more than one occasion. My sister and I, not to be outdone, delivered flyers, sold perfumes, sorted merchandise in a store, and later, as our prospects rose somewhat, tutored students in our respective colleges.

When I was sixteen, my parents worked multiple jobs and so I was the latchkey kid, coming home straight from school, and often bringing the day's entertainment with me. In those days they had video rental stores and VHS cassette tapes that you would pop into a VCR. I can't tell you how many hours I logged in the aisles of the local video stores, especially the adult section. There was a tape there with just the number "10" on it and the image of a seductive young woman walking on the beach, completely naked. Or at least that's what it looked like until you mustered the courage to look intently and discerned that she was clad in a skin-colored swimsuit. How deflating! Well, I finally picked out a movie I liked. I think it was called "Sweet Surrender" or something to that effect. It was a run-of-the mill porno but when you are sixteen it is pure heaven. My two buddies and I started watching it, and after about 10 minutes of it I realized that I never wanted anything so bad in my life as to be shut of these two and watch it all by myself in the privacy of my own home. And the boys were not exactly dolts. One of them said that I was just using my parents' imminent arrival as an excuse to get rid of them so I could gratify my desires after they were gone.

This fascination with the female body only grew as time went by. Had the internet been around when I was growing up, I would doubtless have spent the bulk of my day browsing and consuming pornography. But being a boy of sixteen, I had a fecund imagination. Of course, imagination was no match for reality, when it came to real-world relationships, or the lack thereof. Until senior year of high school I had no girlfriends, quite simply because I did not have the knack for making friends; and also perhaps because I was still adjusting to my new life in a strange land. I was learning the language, although I spoke some English when I came, and simply trying to survive. I was also perhaps a bit of a nerd: playing chess with other kids, studying, being a good boy, and above all being mama's boy. My friend, or so-called friend Naveen, on the other hand, could be seen with a different girl almost every month. And having arrived a year later than me to the country, that was a slap in the face for me. But then he also did some other things in high school that I would never dream of: smoking, drinking, partying to name a few. Reality eventually caught up with him and he became a cab driver, instead of the usual doctor or engineer that he was supposed to become, like all other Indians I know. He hit our car when we were driving somewhere many years later, and on getting out of the car to survey the damage I recognized him right away.

My senior year in high school I sat next to a Jewish girl, Linda, and was utterly infatuated with her. She had long, wavy hair, large bright eyes, and a smile that could make you deliriously happy. I would fantasize about making love to her every night but return to my prim and proper self when sitting next to her during the day. Initially, I was not brave enough to express my feelings for her. The prom was drawing closer every day and the level of anxiety rose proportionally in me as I debated what to do. Finally, I mustered the courage one day when the substitute teacher was reading his newspaper and everyone else was chattering away, to ask her if she would go to the prom with me. She looked surprised for a moment, then smiled and said, "Sure." I was elated. Suddenly, the sun broke through the clouds, and I was bounding like a young lamb.

Soon we started going out on dates on the weekends. At seventeen, my idea of a date was to walk to the nearest bank, get a roll of quarters worth ten dollars, then walk to the bus stop, take a bus to her house, then walk back to the bus stop, pay for her ride as well as mine, and go to this huge diner on Main street called Palace Diner. And palatial it was inside, with neatly arranged tables and pink tablecloths, and a retro jukebox where you would put quarters to play the song of your choice. So you see, if a boy could get his hands on a roll of quarters, he could have a fine time with a pretty girl. In the end it didn't work out, of course, because she found a whiter dude, maybe someone who was also Jewish, albeit a bit younger than her, and just let casually drop to me one day that she would be going with this other guy instead. So I did the logical thing and promptly found myself another girl! Of course, there was no comparison. This other individual was a tiny Indian girl, steeped in her Indian traditions and conservative values; I might as well have gone out with a nun.

It's all poetic justice I suppose, you ask a girl out when the substitute teacher is covering the class, and you end up with a substitute date. Speaking of which, the date was fine. My friend Rupinder and I, along with a bunch of other friends, went to a party on prom night, all dressed up in our rented tuxedos, and danced the early part of the night. We rented the limo, got the corsage, and the whole shebang. After the party we took a cruise around Manhattan, chaperoned of course, with my history teacher following us around all the time. My most vivid memory of the night is standing around in the early morning hours, waiting for something or someone, and my date nervously shifting her weight from one foot to the next. I grew curious and teased that she was still in the mood to dance. She smiled somewhat and confided that she really needed to use the restroom. I looked around and spotted an empty dumpster in the distance and suggested she relieve herself behind it, as I stood guard; but she declined, saying that there would be a very bad smell.

Linda has now moved into my neighborhood! Of course, you can't step into the same river twice: she is married to a Jewish mensch, or so I gather, and has two teenage boys. This being New York City in the 21st century, she is in an apartment building, and I am still living with my parents in their house, so there's none of that stretching out your arms at the green light across the water business. We run into one another sometimes at the grocery store or the bus stop. Sometimes I say hi, sometimes she just ignores me; more often she is simply talking on the phone or has her headphones on. Whatever.

Chapter Eleven

A House of Ill Repute

I have never really understood women, and I believe that has contributed to my premature baldness. I would always get so nervous when conversing with women, likely because I knew the stakes were high in case of failure to impress. For some reason I simply could not capture their imagination! And it was not for lack of trying. I started browsing dating websites in my early twenties, of which there weren't that many back then, and found very little or no response to my overtures. Perhaps I was too young and inexperienced; perhaps I sought the company of women who were too unlike me; perhaps I had never captured the nuances of the intricate dance known as courtship, having had neither mentor nor friend to guide me. Perhaps, as my mother never tires of reminding me, I didn't see enough Hindi movies and learn how to woo Indian women. But you know what, I am not interested in courtship! Just because I am a guy I should run after women, and they should run away and play even harder to get? I don't think so! Call me shallow, but it's just too bad that the overweight women who chase me don't interest me in the least. Everyone's shopping around. There are so many apps and websites now and a deluge of people to swipe left and right on, and so everyone's disposable.

But say you go through the motions. You faithfully and dutifully peruse the websites, contact people, respond to inquiries, talk to them on the phone and even meet them in person. You feel like a broken record: Hi, my name is so and so, I was born here and there, live with my parents (the kiss of death, for some women), have two children from a previous marriage (have I lost you yet?), have no personality whatsoever (you still there?) I like to read (yes, I know it's not very fashionable anymore), go to the office and spend time with my folks over the weekend. How many times and in how many ways do I tell all of this to the revolving door of women that swish in and out of my life faster than the speed of sound?

One day, my co-worker Neal, confided to me that he was considering getting a puppy because all the women swipe right at pictures of men with puppies. This puzzled me because in my mind Neal had all the advantages a guy could hope for: he was good looking, single, with his own place, making good money, a smooth talker and super-friendly! This is not to say he had no shortcomings, but none that were readily apparent to me.

I looked askance at him. "I don't know about that, Neal. At what point do you let on that you really don't have a puppy. I mean, does the puppy grow into a dog at some point and finally die?"

"C'mon man. It's a more visual pick-up line. Don't you go to bars and pick up women?"

"I tell you, Neal, I tried everything man. Heck, let me tell you the story of my life as it relates to women. You wanna hear it?"

He chuckled. "Sure, go for it."

"It all began innocently enough. When the juices started to flow at the onset of puberty, I dutifully smeared the walls with the sap of life. What else was there to do? Then, I think around the time I was in college I began looking in earnest for someone to be with. I don't think I was looking for 'the one.' I don't think I was ever so naïve to believe in the concept of true love and all that, I just wanted someone to spend quality time with, you know. Who the hell wants to be alone? And get this, this was in the early to mid-nineties, so there were no dating apps or smartphones, and the internet was a newborn babe so no real matchmaking websites either. Now, I had just come to this country a few years ago and wasn't really a social animal. No real friends, no networks, living with my parents and going to college, or working during the day when I got my first job and then going home to be with my folks and my sister. No social life whatsoever."

"Well, that sucks!"

"Yeah, tell me about it. And so I started getting this sketchy magazine, called New York. It's come a long way since and is a serious publication now, but back then it was known for its 'massage' advertisements and 'escort services' listings. And you know something, I would get a real thrill out of inquiring about the rates, and discussing logistics with the purveyors of these services, such as when the escort could come to my house, what all she would do and stuff. Of course, they wouldn't want to discuss anything in detail for fear of being caught, but it was such a thrill, man, for a 21-year-old, to call up these women and make arrangements for a good time. It got my heart racing every time!"

He arched his brows. "So, did you actually do it? You called up someone and went for it?"

"No, not quite. Well, it happened, but not in that way. There was like a time bomb ticking in my head. Have you ever heard of women's biological clocks? How they are always saying, hey my time is running out. I gotta get a kid soon?"

"Sure, who hasn't?"

"Well, it was a little bit like that with me. I kept getting more and more anxious and nervous and desperate. I was twenty-two or almost twenty-three, had a job that hardly paid anything since it was my first job out of college, and was living with my folks. And so one day I made some pretense to attend a parade or something in Manhattan and took off to visit—oh, how shall I say? --A house of ill repute. And boy, what a place! Just a whole bunch of skimpily clad Chinese women of all sizes, a roomful of them, staring at me. I was paralyzed with visceral terror, but then someone looked into my eyes and said slowly but emphatically, 'Just choose one. We are all very nice!' I picked one, but she had just been with a client and wanted to sleep. Then I picked another and she took me by the hand and into a room no bigger than a closet, with a single bed and a red lamp on a small nightstand. She closed the door, leaving it ajar, and promised to return in a few minutes. She was so lithe, shapely, and athletic: a pleasure to look at.

"When she had stepped out an older woman peered in and looked me over up and down and shook her head. I mean, just shook her head and said, 'tsk, tsk.' Crazy, right? Well, I couldn't really care less at that moment, because I was bursting at the seams to get this done with. I can't remember being so focused and with such a clear sense of purpose ever before in my life.

"So guess what, the lady comes back and starts getting undressed. I ask nervously, 'You have a condom, right?' She laughs and says I have a great sense of humor! But first financial arrangements need to be made. She says it will be $200 with a $50 tip for an hour. I take out the money from my left sock, carefully count it and hand it to her. It is exactly $200. I lie and say that's all I have. Next thing I know I am on top, and she is going at it full tilt right below me. Suddenly she flips and is now lying on her stomach. I slow down for a minute because I never knew that could be done physically, and don't understand how she did it, but even as I am considering this, she flips back again and is now on her back.

"After I come and we are lying on the bed, she takes some tissues and wipes me clean. She asks, 'Feel better?' I nod and stare in space. My brain is steeped in a multitude of emotions: confusion, attachment, regret, guilt. Everything is so hazy and surreal. The great mystery of coitus has just been solved. This is how it is done."

Neal gave me a bemused look. "That's some story! You know, it's funny how women think they are smarter than men."

"Yeah, so what? Everyone thinks they are smarter than everyone else."

"But you see, there's a reason why they think so, and maybe they are right. You know I think I've figured it out. You see, all day we guys are in suits and ties, and most guys in offices are in ties–"

"Not really, the culture is changing dude. They are wearing sneakers and sport coats and going tieless. Maybe back in the--"

"Stop interrupting me, Ajay, for fuck's sake! I meant in our line of work. I know what's going on. Anyway, as I was saying, we are in these ties that are choking the blood circulation to our necks all the time, and so hardly any blood is circulating up to our heads. And then we see these beautiful women with their low-cut blouses, especially in the summertime and nice long legs, and what blood we have remaining goes in the opposite direction from our heads! And then they say, we think with our dicks. Hellooo!"

"Very well observed, my man. I never thought of it like that. And I guess I now know why."

Neal checked his watch. "I think we should be heading back to the office."

Chapter Twelve

Ladies Man

So, how did I descend to such depravity that I started consorting with hookers?" I don't know. I mean, it wasn't always like this. When I was in elementary school in India, I was too shy to even think about the other sex. I used to sit in the classroom with my best friend, and at lunchtime he and I would sit under our desks and eat our lunches, the relative privacy of this space a welcome respite from the hustle and bustle of the classroom. When I went to middle school, I had loosened up a bit, and all my efforts were carefully calibrated to get noticed by this Americanized girl, Priya Marwaha, the least Indian-looking specimen in the entire school. And then in high school I made some more progress by sitting next to girls and holding a conversation with them.

In college, I used to stay up till 3 a.m. sometimes talking to a girl who insisted that the lettuce she was eating in her sandwich was once alive and well and was now about as good as dead meat. And once when we were sitting and eating lunch under a shady tree in the summertime, and after I had had just enough of this kind of talk and wanted to change the subject, she gave me such a look that I instantly felt like a low-life. "What's the matter?" I asked, and she told me about a book she was reading, *Girl, Interrupted* and how it was all about guys interrupting girls and "man-splaining" and "man-spreading" and all that kind of nonsense. And I remember thinking to myself, look, all I really want to do is get with you! I don't care about any of this lettuce with its veins and its karma and after-life and new-age feminist stuff. Don't you get it? And I am too debonair to just put it to you crassly. Oh well, if only it were that easy.

So college comes and goes, and like I said to Neal, I had this fifty-pound time bomb ticking in my head, going "I gotta get laid, I gotta get laid" that was driving me nuts. So I just went ahead and did it. What's there to it? Never mind the cooties and the bright red spots on my nuts that burned like hellfire for days on end. It's all part of the experience, right? Maybe the worst part of it wasn't even that. It was perhaps the remorseful realization that I threw it all away so cheaply. That for even the space of an hour I got emotionally involved with a sex worker, and didn't want to let her go, as she gently closed the door on my face after our time was up.

After all this, after all such difficulties in developing meaningful, sustainable, real relationships with women, after all the years chasing them down, to Australia, England, Europe, India and lord knows perhaps even to other planets had interplanetary travel been an option in those days, I resigned myself to the fates and the furies, aka arranged marriages. I tried to prevent it, to convince my parents that this was really not for me. After my affair with Ruby, the Filipina, I was, in fact, totally against it. The affair kind of just happened all by itself as it were. After talking online for a few days, one afternoon just as I was wrapping up work, I went to an online chat room and started chatting with her. She announced, much to my delight, that she was coming to the U.S. in two months. After she arrived, we met up in a restaurant and talked for hours. She had a lithe body, slim and shapely, shoulder-length black hair, and a bit of a protruding jawline. She wasn't particularly attractive, and I would say not even above-average, but as they say, a bird in hand . . . I then proposed to her that she take a little trip with me to Philly.

She hesitated. "Orient me a little. Where is Philly, relative to NY?"

Funny, I thought, that she should say "orient" given that she was from the orient.

I took two used up napkins and put one on top of the other. "There you go! See, it's really close by. Just two hours from the city. We can explore the city, shop, etc." and my voice trailed off a bit at the "etc." because we both knew, I imagine, what the et cetera could be.

Ruby Pearl. What a girl, I tell you! The first night was hard. It was Sunday, the first of January, and the next day I had to go to work. So while getting some rest would have been nice, I had other competing priorities and was working hard to persuade her to give herself entirely to me. Well I never got to the "entirely" part, actually, because I kept hearing things like, "Oh, I am just not ready yet," "No, please, stop. What are you doing?" to which my ready reply was, "Massaging you, of course!" So she had her "massage" in her nether regions from my fingers but never let it progress much beyond that. By morning my eyes looked like grape tomatoes, and I was exhausted from all that fruitless exertion. So I got dressed and went to work. After an hour or so at work I felt jetlagged and don't quite recall just how I made it for the next seven hours, but staggered back to my hotel room in the evening and crashed on the bed for the night, too tired even to go out for dinner. I wish I still had that card that she left me: so thoughtfully and lovingly written, strewn with flower petals and beautiful drawings, thanking me and professing her love for me. She had gone shopping at the Market Street mall adjoining the Westin where we were staying, bought the card, and placed it at the table for me. I read it and immediately tore it to pieces, muttering "Evidence, evidence. You are not going to get me like that." What was I supposed to do, take the card home to my parents and show it to them proudly?

The next time we met in San Francisco I noticed she had changed somewhat. She was more easy-going. She confided to me that she had almost been raped a few weeks ago when someone she knew invited her over to his house, got her drunk and almost pushed himself on her. She had found the strength and the will somehow to escape him. She didn't report him, being a recent immigrant who did not want to cause a stir, and because in her mind no crime had been committed. She relayed all this to me slowly and hesitatingly and seemed as if she were beseeching me to forgive her. "Good!" I thought. Serves you right for refusing my advances. Now you will have more appreciation for someone who actually respects a woman's wishes. And indeed she had! We made love repeatedly in that swanky hotel room in the W Hotel by the bay. It did not hurt that I had surprised her by inviting myself into the bathroom as she showered. Initially her reaction had been one of panic and shock and she hastened to cover herself up and disengage. I feigned offense and went back to bed to watch TV. After showering she came to me and tried to placate me. When that didn't work she kissed me on the lips and started tugging at my briefs. I put on my favorite CD, one of Yanni's numbers, and we went to work.

By the morning when we left to explore the city we both felt a bit of a pain in our genitals. That was a surprise to me. I was expecting to feel alive, fulfilled, rejuvenated. I realized soon that I had strained some muscles that I did not exercise daily. She found ways to cling to me more and more now: at the sight of dogs, since she was terrified of them; near the water, since she was afraid of falling in; on the cliffs of Highway 1, since she was afraid of heights; and so on. I loved it. My very first girlfriend ever! And yet, if only her face had been as beautiful as her body was lithe! I dared not look at her too much in public, though, for I felt the eyes of other women who would scrutinize Ruby to try to understand me and then walk away unimpressed.

Who can argue with one's member though? Here was a young, nubile girl, ready and willing, purportedly in love with me, and so who was I to interfere in such a beautiful thing and complicate matters to my own detriment? A few months later, I was working in Birmingham, Alabama, and cursing myself out daily, swearing aloud that if I marry it would be a wage-earning, professional woman, because damn it, earning a living was just so hard! Harder still, of course, when you are on an IT project and don't know coding or any of the other technical skills the job demands.

I was hanging on for the perks: new car rentals every week, hotel points and airline miles, per-diem for meals and expenses. You know, the good life! Of course, I couldn't keep this going for long, but somewhere in the midst of all that drudgery it occurred to me that I could also get an apartment there, like some of my other colleagues, and try an experiment in solo living. And while I was on my own, why not bring my girl over?

And so I did! I sent her a ticket and she promised to pay me back a portion of it when we met; I didn't really need the money but wanted her to have some skin in the game. Later that day, I found myself at the local Victoria's Secret, looking sheepishly in the aisles. An older woman, observing me closely, divined my intentions and before long I was on my way with a package of intimates for my visitor. After I picked her up from the airport we dined at one of the trendier restaurants in downtown Birmingham, an Indian joint popular with the locals. It was the best option at the time, given that the downtown in those days had a total of three skyscrapers and large parts of it seemed deserted and sketchy. Then we drove back to the apartment. Ruby was tired but agreed to try on her new lingerie. She wore it to please me but complained that it suffocated her because the bra was biting into her ribs. And so I turned down the lights and peeled off her clothes.

"You look so tired from your trip, baby!"

"Being with you gives me energy."

"Sure, that's how you get your protein!"

"Ha! Ha! Very funny. You are the vegan, remember?

"Vegetarian, but I will eat you all the same!"

At first we tried the recliner, with her legs around my neck, but then my knees started hurting and it was getting boring, not to mention disgusting to keep eating her and pretending to enjoy it. So I perched her on the dining room table and slid right into her. Pure ecstasy. Suddenly everything fell away: all cares, worries, trepidations. I was instantly transported to another world. This is the meaning of life, I thought. This is my purpose; this is what I had been seeking all along.

When we woke up in the morning it was more of the same. I had bought a carton of condoms, not knowing how many I would need, and now I admired my forethought. We were in bed for a long time; sometimes she was on top, sometimes flat on her back, sometimes doggy style. Eventually, it became just too much work. By the time we got into the car so she could catch her flight, I was winded, and she could barely walk. Halfway to the airport she groaned audibly and closed her eyes. A panic set in my mind. What if she died? How would I explain that to the police and to my parents? I parked outside a restaurant and told her to hang on and got some mozzarella sticks and some cheese and crackers. "Thank you," she said, but didn't touch it. She revealed later that she suffered from low blood sugar, and going at it all morning without eating had depleted her to the point of exhaustion. We met a few more times after that in different cities in the U.S., given that leaving the country was not possible for her due to her visa restrictions.

Once, she gave me a blank check with just her signature, and I took every opportunity to show it to my friends and brag about the trust she had placed in me. I cashed it for just half the amount she had suggested. It wasn't about the money after all. But given that it wasn't love either, it didn't work out. To her credit, she tried: asking me repeatedly if she could meet my parents, calling me to ask about "us," but I wasn't having it.

How could I? She was not beautiful!

Chapter Thirteen

To Have and Have Not

Not long after Ruby had graduated from my clutches, I found Anjali. Now the time with Anjali was a fine time since she was in Florida, and I was dating a girl from New Jersey as well. Her name was Gemini, and I remember that because of this diner in Midtown Manhattan that bears the same name.

Anjali was from the south of India, a scrawny girl with a dark complexion, flat-chested, small, with curly hair. We spoke on the phone a few times and I thought I was getting away with murder when once again I proposed that we meet and then take a road trip together to Miami, and lo and behold, she agreed! I couldn't believe my luck. So I flew down to Orlando, picked her up and off we went. She was wearing a rather skimpy dress, and my hand had no trouble landing on her knee. She smiled coyly and put her hand on top of mine. We stopped at a rest stop and then at a beach. Soon we were on the beach, rolling on the sand, kissing.

Anjali looked at me with playful eyes. "What we really needed was a bedroom, not the beach."

I laughed in assent as we made our way back to the rental, a gray compact just big enough for the two of us.

Back at the hotel she told me that many guys don't like to "do" girls when they are menstruating, but it was up to me. Given how breathtakingly close I was to my goal, I thought nothing of it and we went at it. I still remember looking down at my pecker afterward to see it all smeared with blood. That was a scary sight all right, and I promised myself to never go back to such shenanigans. It's amazing how quickly one comes to one's senses and regains the ability to think after discharging one's load.

I don't know if it's funny or sad that I don't remember much about her—her family, her goals, aspirations, dreams, habits... nothing! Except, of course, how dark her skin looked against mine in the late afternoon light that slanted in from the thin hotel drapes; how she vigorously and conscientiously sucked me so that I had a devil of a time controlling my laughter, even during the fact. Once, of course, as she was so dutifully engaged, I let my mind drift and came without telling her. She suddenly stopped and said, "Oh, you came!" Well, duh!

We went to Key Biscayne the following day, just drove around really, and ate at a restaurant, with no clear purpose. The trip was uneventful except for the time she wanted to take a selfie with both of us in it, and I resented it, of course, but said nothing. The next day was the beach. The sun nearly blinded me as we approached the sand dunes. Just as we started walking toward the beach, I received a phone call from the brother of another girl I was talking to in Texas. This one had six toes; that seemed to be her defining feature. I let Anjali walk in front of me as I conversed with the brother, discussing logistics for my upcoming visit to Houston to see his sister. Anjali looked at me askance and I hurriedly said goodbye to the brother, not wanting to risk discovery and thus our arrangement. There was a topless girl on the beach, waving her arms in the air, taking in the sunshine, dipping her feet in the tide, and doing cartwheels. With some effort I averted my eyes from her when I saw Anjali glaring at me. Later that night she asked me about the phone call, and I made some nonsensical reply, too sleepy to bother.

Once back in New York, life settled into a routine. Anjali wrote me a nasty email once I reimbursed her for part of her expenses since we were not going to be together. I knew that was coming, but I really didn't care since I had started seeing Gemini on the weekends, and was quite happy with the way things were progressing. My only regret, ultimately, was that while I came tantalizingly close, I never actually got to fool around with Gemini after all. She was a few years my junior and in perfect shape, with a devious smile and a quick mind; and, alas regrettably, elusive as hell. Her Achilles' heel was her face—marred by splotches and innumerable pockmarks and pustules. Almost like the lunar surface, you might say. You name the remedy, and she had already tried it, from the mundane to the esoteric. I liked to think this was the face that launched a thousand ships—*away* from her! And so she was shopping around, with the tick tock of the proverbial clock in her ears, but perhaps willing to settle for someone like me. Once or twice, when I was in the middle of something, she would tease me about my potbelly or my receding hairline or being able to see the wax in my right ear. Humiliated and angry, I almost lost it and nearly lashed out at her. I remember the overnight trip we took together to Philadelphia. There must have been something there between us, since she did not hesitate to sleep in the same bed as me. Of course, sleep was the furthest thing from my mind in the middle of the night. So, naturally, soon as I figured that she was fast asleep, I went to work on her pajama drawstrings.

This woke her up and she sat up abruptly.

"What are you trying to do? Don't you see that I am sleeping?"

Mortified, I stammered, "Ju-- just, trying to caress you, that's all."

She gave a faint smile, then dropped back onto the mattress and turned over. "Don't bother me now. I am sleeping."

The next day, my desires still unfulfilled and eyes heavy with sleep, I got behind the wheel for the return trip to New York. But as it turned out, all was not in vain. This episode had shown her that I liked her, and she was more receptive to my advances. We would sit in the car smooching for what seemed like eternity many a day, until I had an epiphany: why not book a motel room near my house? So that's what I did but couldn't bring myself to inform her until we were in the car and riding towards our destination. To my surprise she did not protest all that much. She simply said that she had never done something like this before, and I vehemently agreed that neither had I. At the motel we wasted no time trying to take off each other's clothes. And of course, as I was busy with this, Anjali had to call just then. Such impeccable timing! Fortunately, the phone was on vibrate so I took a quick glance and silenced it. We caressed, fully naked, and then I suggested we take a shower. More caressing in the shower, but still no progress. A part of me was afraid of mounting her, or rather having her mount me in the slippery tub and breaking my neck. So she made some excuse soon enough and got dressed and we left, rather abruptly to my liking.

So this also ended. What of it? I figured. There will be others; there always are.

Chapter Fourteen

The Son Also Rises

Soon after filing for custody I also filed for divorce. But, as my attorney had explained earlier, there is no such thing without squaring off about money and kids first. The kid part got resolved, it seems, because Maya's attorney convinced her that her chances of winning custody of both children, or even of the child in her possession, were slim given that she was in temporary housing, with no education, no training, and no job. Of course, I had no inkling of it at that time: our attorney never took the time to explain the same and we were so focused on just hanging on to what we had that we did not think critically or strategically. Just the thought of losing my girl was enough to spark a panic in me and so I never expanded my horizons to anything beyond that. Now that that was behind us, it became all about money. I was trying to hang on to what I had, and she wanted it all. Through all the negotiations, the back and forth, the business about childcare costs, the length of spousal support, equitable distribution, and each party's correct burden for unreimbursed medical expenses, a single thing haunted me: what about my boy? Was he going to be a subway performer, gyrating his hips and swinging from the pole on the E train for a few bucks? Or was he on the school-to-prison pipeline?

And so it turned out that the boy was a bigger deal than I ever realized. Every time I would talk to a woman for the purposes of fornication or friendship, I would be hard pressed to explain to her that I had my daughter with me full-time and my ex had my son the entire time; that the kids never saw each other or played together; that hundreds of dollars flowed like an eternal spring to my ex every month, supposedly to support this little egg and his serpent-like keeper, who had coiled herself over him; that the toxic sludge in our hearts had hardened to such a degree that undoubtedly the mother was poisoning the son against the father; that the father was essentially doing the same, albeit so much more subtly since he was more educated and refined etc. But what I could not do, what I could never bring myself to say, was that I was powerless to do anything *about* the boy and *for* the boy.

"You can always go to court, you know," someone would invariably say.

"Of course, I can," I would rejoin, "But to what end? The courts don't want to do anything. Really, they don't. What will they say? Okay, since the kids are under 13 or 14 or whatever, they should go to counseling or family therapy or what have you. Who wants that? Might as well sit in a can of shit eight hours a day. I am sure that would be more pleasant. Heck, the lawyer I had retained for custody a few years ago was just running from courtroom to courtroom, shoving food into his mouth. And so no wonder he would look shell-shocked when I accosted him about his lack of follow through. I wrote you an email and left you a voicemail more than a week ago, but never heard back from you, I would say. And he would just offer a perfunctory apology and reiterate how busy he was, as always.

One day, Neal and I were taking our customary stroll in the delightful environs of cosmopolitan Long Island City, checking out the new restaurants in the area. He looked at me thoughtfully.

"Why don't you file for custody of your boy?"

"Well, I have been advised against it by my attorney."

"Why would he do that? Doesn't he make more money if you file?"

"Ha, ha! Yes, of course he does, but he and I both know the chances of actually winning custody are slim to none."

"Then, what do you plan to do?"

"See, that's the problem Neal. What can you do, really? I really don't want to expose my daughter to that loose woman and her ways. Who knows where she lives, what she does, who she sees! To her, lying is as natural as breathing. What kind of influence would she have on my child? If I say I want to see Kash—"

"Your son?"

"Yes. Even if I see my son for two hours every weekend, then I am running every single weekend, more or less, to visit him: in Brooklyn, Manhattan, you name it. And then, of course, she will also say that she wants to meet the girl for the same amount of time, if not longer. Because, after all, these are just chess pieces for her. She doesn't really care about her kids. I am not sure she even sees them as people."

"What makes you say that? They are her kids too, aren't they?"

"Yeah, technically, but not emotionally. Heck, she is just using the boy to enrich herself. If she cared about him she would give him to me. I earn so much more than her, I have my parents to help with childcare, and I can teach them something. But no! Who cares about the kids? Not her. So, anyway, say I meet up with Kash two hours or so a week. What's that going to do for him? Or me? I know what it will do for me: it will make me even sadder and make me grieve more for him. How is that helpful? I will feel helpless and depressed."

"So, hold on. You don't want to see your son so that your ex doesn't get to see her daughter?"

"I am a bad man, right? That's what you want to say? Huh, Neal?"

"Hey man, it's none of my business, you know."

"But you are right. That's really it. Now, I know that I cannot get custody of the boy if he won't spend any time with me and doesn't even know me. And she knows that too, so she is playing the same game as me! In fact, for her it is probably worse. I brought Kash home for two hours last year. He didn't want to leave. I pretty much pushed him off to his mother and ran away, and even then he didn't really want to go with her. The scene has haunted me ever since. That was then of course. Now, it seems she has brainwashed the boy, and he is scared of coming with me."

"Maybe you should think this through and take it one step at a time. Just build a rapport with the kid and try to be in his life as much as possible. At least, that's what I would do."

"Yeah, that makes sense. It really does. It sounds good, you know. But like I said, what will two hours every week do for me or him? Now, you can make the same argument for my daughter and say that if she spends two hours with her mother every week it won't be the end of the world, and I see that, but I have an almost visceral fear of losing her. I am afraid that she will be corrupted by her mother, so you might say that I just sacrificed one child for the sake of another. That boy is finished, he really is. I cannot help him; I can just watch helplessly as he is ravaged by the forces arrayed against him: an economically depressed outlook, systemic oppression, an unsympathetic mother, various diseases and ailments . . . the works. What influence can I possibly have on him in such a short amount of time? It's fruitless. But you know what? It's not for lack of trying. I told the woman to come and meet with her daughter, but no, she wanted a mid-point between Queens and Brooklyn. I said screw it; I will meet you at the Carousel in Forest Park, or even at the bloody mall right outside of Brooklyn. Heck, it's four miles from your house. But no sir! She won't have it: it's too far from public transportation; it's not near my house; I insist on meeting at the library in Long Island City or at the Sikh Temple in Richmond Hill. C'mon! Take a cab if you must; have a friend drive you. I am traveling almost ten miles to come and see you. Have you no shame? No, she never had any shame as far back as I can remember. Even before we were married she used to ask me to insert some medicine using a syringe into her pussy! Can you believe it? She would pretend to be unable to see where to insert it herself or how to do it and ask me to do it; at first I was excited, of course, just as she had figured, but when it became tiresome day after day, and she clearly saw the annoyance on my face, she said never mind and started doing it herself. The whore! Whore of Babylon!"

"Get a hold of yourself, man! Jesus Christ!"

"Sorry, dude. Didn't mean to subject you to such venting. I need to calm down."

Chapter Fifteen

After Great Pain, A Formal Feeling Comes

I remember when my divorce was finalized and the time right before it. Just a few months before it was all said and done, I was sitting in my majestic office with the door closed. It was a long, rectangular room, with just one more desk for another guy who shared the space with me. A few weeks ago this guy got a job somewhere else, so now I had the place to myself. I had sauntered in at my customary time of 9:30 a.m. or maybe it was 10 o'clock. Who cares? It was a bright, clear day with blue skies and high clouds. I was on the phone with my attorney and we were discussing the numbers for the final settlement. The wretch wanted more than her due, of course, and kept tacking on, tacking on, until my temples throbbed, and I felt I would explode, with my insides splattering the walls. So we talked about how to fudge the numbers. In the end it didn't work because she wouldn't budge from her own figures; and all this time I was paying child support and alimony and the lawyer, on top of all my other regular monthly expenses, so I basically just lay down and died.

Going to court was akin to smoking without exhaling. My heart thumped louder as I went through security, and even more so as I got ushered in the courtroom. My chest tightened and I drew shallow breaths as I swore to tell the truth, and nothing but the truth, over and over again, without really uttering more than a sentence or two, if that. You can't really speak your mind in a courtroom. You must let the lawyers do the talking, or your goose is cooked. And then there were the long waits, with both parties retreating to their respective corners to plot against the other, the lawyers meeting by themselves in the middle to hash out the details and maybe even collude, for all I knew. And always there was one thing or another: a backlog of cases so that you were left to rot in the hallway, one of the attorneys running late, what with four attorneys—two for us and two for each of the kids, and the magical, elusive chimera known as the Punjabi interpreter, who may or may not show up! Once all the planets were aligned and these dignitaries in attendance, court would be in session.

If only it ended there! As soon as you turned the key into the latch and opened your front door, you got to relive it all with your parents. You had to recount, memory by morbid memory, the unsavory details of what transpired in the courtroom. Who said what, who argued how, who looked askance at which precise moment, and what the lawyer said, and the judge implied, and the Punjabi interpreter misinterpreted. Then I would drag my carcass up the steps to my room and glare at the quote that adorned my bedroom wall:

Were I from Dunsinane away and clear,
Profit again should hardly draw me here.

There would also be times when on a single day there would be two court visits, one on the second floor and one on the fifth. One to settle the finances, and one to deal with the lingering issue of visitations. And that meant two swearing in ceremonies to tell the truth, and nothing but the truth. Nothing like it to make one feel like Gandhi. So the wench finally did a handwritten job, via her lawyer, to draw up some articles of visitation wherein both parties would agree to finding a mutually agreeable place to hold the visitations, do FaceTime, and God knows what else claptrap, to put an end to this courtroom drama. I signed, of course, because the document was so absurd that not signing it would have made me doubt my sanity. It had no binding legal force, as there were no attestations made or something like that. I couldn't care less. But Madam sure did. After we made it out of the courtroom, the emails started bouncing back and forth between the attorneys. They would invariably begin with "my client proposes," or something to that effect, that the parties commence visitations in a library in Long Island City, or in a Sikh Temple in Richmond Hill or in a Dunkin Donuts in Brooklyn, which to me was the edge of the world! And for each location that she and her attorney proposed, I would respond, as my attorney, and suggest another location more convenient for me. The Queens Center Mall by this time was out of the question for her, given that she had practically been forced to go there every weekend, to abide by the temporary court order a few months ago, and so she probably hated the place.

Since there was no other option, I sought advice from the only person I might confide in. "So what do you think, Neal?"

"Well, how about you just make an agreement with her for the sake of making an agreement and then make excuses, you know, like oh I am busy today, have a dental appointment, a flat tire. Something like that."

"Well, you can't do that Neal, because you have to abide by the letter of the law, if not the spirit."

"You think they are going to follow you around and enforce the law. C'mon man, the court don't care. Once they do their thing they pretty much leave you alone, unless you are flagrantly disregarding the order."

"But here's the thing, see. Here's the dilemma I told you about earlier. I miss the boy. I want to see the boy. He is my son; he is a part of me. My heart goes out to him. I want him to succeed, to become someone, to further the legacy of our family. In Indian culture, the boy is everything. He is the one who moves the dynasty forward, brings recognition and honor to the family, and is the bearer of the torch, so to speak. But it's not just the social aspect, it is the moral and ethical morass: I pay good money for the kid every month, yet I have no contact with him. I am his father but have no influence on him; I can help the kids of hundreds of other parents via my work in the school system, but not my own."

"Wait a second! Didn't we have this discussion or something similar just a few months ago? When you lost all control and started calling your ex names?"

"Maybe, but I really need your advice on this Neal, given that—"

"You can't have your cake and eat it too. Seems to me that you want to do all this for your boy because he is your boy, but don't want your ex to do anything for your daughter."

"Why do you say that?"

"Well, listen to you. If you do all this for your son, wouldn't your wife want to spend some time with her daughter too? Are you okay with that?"

"Honestly, no. She is a bad influence, a bad actor, a pernicious presence. You name it! I don't want my daughter to be subjected to her values or the lack thereof. Why do you think we divorced? I didn't want anything from my ex. I didn't stand to get any alimony. Shit, come to think of it, she mentioned alimony in our very first meeting back in India, and I thought to myself, heck, this is weird to be discussing this the first time you meet someone, and I didn't pay any attention to the writing on the wall."

"Any chance the two of you can patch it up between you?"

"Zero percent. Are you kidding? It's been four years since we got divorced. And boy, that divorce was hard fought and won, I tell you. But I did it, I had to do it for my little girl. She was suffering at the hands of her own mother, for crying out loud!"

"So, what are you going to do now?"

"I don't want to go back to court but maybe that's the only option. I know, I know, we just got out of court, but this situation is so untenable you know. I gotta find a way to see my son—"

"Without letting your ex see your daughter."

"Exactly. It's terrible, right? But I gotta find a way, somehow."

Even though I knew better, having gone over all possible ways the custody case could and probably would go wrong, I was thinking of advancing the deposit to my lawyer so he could get the ball rolling. But then one afternoon I came home from work and saw my mom curled up on the sofa, in debilitating pain, moaning and groaning. Dad explained that she had eaten an unripe mango the night before, against her better judgment.

So the next few days were spent at the hospital. When informed that this was her third hospitalization in as many years, the doctor was impressed.

"Really?" he blurted. "That's very good, actually. Many patients come every couple of months."

Such a winsome bedside manner! I thought. Here lies my mother on this sterile hospital bed, with the nasogastric tube coming out of her nose, unable to speak much, half drowsy from all the drugs in her system, nauseous and in excruciating pain, and this is the encouragement she receives?

One day went by, then two, then three. My mother got shuffled around from room to room. The doctors and nurses kept reminding me that should things not improve, they would have to resort to surgery. Meanwhile, my mother had had enough. She insisted that she was feeling better, yanked the tube out of her nose, after several requests when no one bothered to do it for her, and just put her foot down. There was still no discharging her from the hospital though. The doctors wanted to ensure she could pass stool.

As I waited by her bedside that night, half-asleep, a sinister morbidity crept over me. You repress yourself enough, and it works, I thought! Soon, you no longer feel the urge to write or express your emotions. In time, you are no different than the chair across the room or the rug under your feet! Just a shell of a man, with a veneer of respectability, devoid of ambition, urges, feelings. More an automaton, a provider, a medium through which financial resources flow to merchants and businesses. Is this where all my musings on existence have finally led me? To this barren, arid land of meaninglessness? Life, like everything else, begs to be organized, sorted, dealt with, so it is not simply an amalgamation of fragmented experiences, images, and random happenstance. Or worse, perhaps, a series of chores to be completed before kicking the bucket! Surely we mean more, matter more, aspire higher than a mundane existence. Here lies the woman who raised me, sacrificed her life to elevate mine and to give me the opportunities she herself did not have, and here she withers away now in this inhospitable hospital.

Chapter Sixteen

Of Fathers and Sons

And when our troubles come, they come not as single spies but in droves. My dad decided shortly after mom's discharge that now was as good a time as any to go in for open-heart surgery. Goaded on by his profit-seeking physicians and terrified of becoming incapacitated like his elder brother, dad sought out an elective procedure that could conceivably make him unable to recover at his advanced age.

Upon reflection, I never understood my father to the extent I would have liked. He wavered many times and was laconic, pensive, and reticent. That was the impression one usually got of him. But peel back this persona and there was a dormant energy that scrutinized every utterance, uncovered the unspoken assumptions, and explored possibilities that might not have been considered by the speaker. He listened to me attentively and open-mindedly enough, and when I had finished, he sat with it and searched his being: was it true for him? Did it square with his experience of the world? We ate together mostly but he almost always ate in silence, never initiating the conversation and responding only for the sake of decorum. He was a layered man, always ready with a joke or an anecdote to illustrate the point he wanted to make. But I never felt I peeled back enough to get to his core—to really know him and understand what made him tick. But perhaps that was easier said than done. Every day he went deeper and deeper within his own mind, meditating and listening to satsang--the spiritual discourse, not the band-- for four or five hours each day, so that he was hardly present for even half the time in this world as the rest of us. And even when he was on the same plane of consciousness, he was rushing to dispatch his own affairs: paying bills, shopping, and doing chores around the house before his next meditation session began. So, in a sense he was the true karma yogi, always engaged in action, but never interested in the fruits thereof. While he was mostly disinterested and dispassionate, there were notable exceptions: politics, mathematics, and anything concerning his daughter. Father and daughter had a mental and spiritual bond so that no criticism of either would register in the other's psyche, and the two could converse for hours no matter the topic. If it had not been for the difference in their ages, one could be forgiven for thinking they were a couple.

In this quest to really know my father, I reflected on what I knew about *his* father—my grandfather. Dadaji, as he was referred to reverently, was a rather gaunt, stick-like figure, almost to the point of emaciation. He loved dabbling in homeopathic medicines and doling out little sweet pills to all the kids in the extended family. And as a kid, I was game for anything sweet, so I particularly enjoyed those moments. Dadaji was a man who had seen much in life and supposedly accomplished even more. He had been in government service as a tax collector, started a textile factory, and ultimately died during a prayer ceremony at a Sikh temple. I cannot say I really knew grandpa as a person— I saw him only sporadically whenever dad would take the whole family to visit him in Ludhiana. We would take the express train —the Sher-E-Punjab, or the lion of Punjab, and after a few hours find ourselves in narrow cobblestone alleys with drains on either side. Muddy waters ran down those drains from the assorted houses that lined them. From the outside, Grandpa's house looked quite ordinary. Inside, after passing through the massive, wooden double doors, one came across a few rusty old bicycles in the corner and then the narrow passage opened up to a huge courtyard, with an assortment of flooring—cobblestones on one part, concrete on the other, but mostly mud as one ventured to the far side near the latrines.

As dad's large family came and greeted him, the cacophony of voices was punctuated by barking and tail thumping noises. Rosie, the family dog chained to her post, would join in the excitement. Rosie was a rather capricious canine. I remember seeing her hairy, uplifted chin, and dark brown apso eyes staring steadily at me, her tail wagging vigorously; and, as I approached, suddenly she would start barking, growling, and baring her worn brittle teeth. She had a less-than-ideal puppyhood. My cousins, Raju and Sonu, would hang her upside down by her tail, toss her around, and commit other atrocities. Being that there was no manual on dog abuse, they had to improvise for the most part. So, in time, Rosie learned to cope. Vengeance was hers! And I, being just a boy of eight or nine in those days, reminded her of her early days and out came her rotting teeth to ward off little urchins like me.

∞∞∞

So now, it was our turn to care for dad. I would be exhausted by work, childcare, and the emotional uncertainty of not knowing what to expect and when. Would he recover? Succumb? How much time and effort should I put into the upkeep of his health? My mother and sister behaved at times as if these were his last days and tortured me with their stares and blunt rebukes when they saw me leave for work. Who will care for Iris, they would say? It's your responsibility. Our primary responsibility is toward our father and husband, not caring for your child. That is all you, now. So I stayed home or brought Iris to the hospital. The day of the surgery was the longest. I must have logged thousands of steps that day, pacing back and forth in the hallway outside the emergency room, and then the intensive care unit. Finally, dad showed some signs of progress, and we could all go home. The year that followed tried us all. I was waking up in the bluish-dark before dawn and dropping off Iris to school. Sometimes I would rush back in the middle of the day to pick her up before her school bus arrived and in doing so lose half a day of work. My greatest fear was to be labeled a slacker at work and suffer the looks of derision from my peers and my boss.

Slowly, though, dad recovered somewhat, and he was able to do the afternoon pickups. That's when I realized how dependent I was on my parents. Without them, I couldn't report to work, or if at work, focus on work for fear of running late for pickups. After-school programs were no panacea either. It was not just their cost, but the quality of care. To compound it all, Iris was a vegetarian, like all of us, and had no access to healthful food that also appealed to her palate. More and more, every day, my dream of reuniting with my son, via a long, drawn-out custody battle, became just that: a distant dream. For some time now, I had not spoken to him or seen him. Sometimes I wondered if he was still alive. Oftentimes I was gripped by confusion and uncertainty. My brain started branching out all the different scenarios. If he is indeed alive, in what health? Who cares for him? Will he talk to me or even know who I am? Does he know the meaning of words like father, mother, brother, or sister? Last I saw him, he was five years old and called me "Fador." What is a *fador*? Is he not a father? Is he a failed father? A father who has abandoned his child? These are matters of the heart. Then there are more practical matters. Matters of the brain. If my son dies then I can finally save some money. I will grieve for him, sure, but consolation would be easy since we were essentially strangers. But if we are just strangers, why does it pain me that I cannot see him or help him in my own way? Why do I feel for him? Why not just call him Bill, since that is all he is to me, a bill you receive in the mail, and pay it and be done with it? Do I feel so strongly about my utility bills? Do I agonize over the health of the strangers who send me my credit card statement? So no, he is not just a bill to be paid, he is a human being, and I fear the worst for him. And yet I am powerless to help him.

Ultimately, I got tired of procrastinating and decided to call Kash. Sure enough, there he was on the other end of the line, very much alive. I asked him if he knew who he was speaking to and he said, "my dad." And as I heard those words, a pang of shame and remorse rippled through me. I asked him about his schooling and how he was spending his summer vacation, and he answered them dutifully. Then, when I asked if he wanted to speak with his sister, he readily agreed. The two video-conferenced, and flipping his phone's camera, Kash showed us the view from his apartment, perched high above the city. All in all, he seemed happy, unconcerned with the exigencies of our family situation which led us to lead separate lives and put no hard questions to me. But, then again, he was not even eight years old at the time.

Sometimes I think I just made up all manner of excuses so I could feel better about myself. Like the time I went on a date with Alka, the physician from Connecticut. And of course, since it was our first date, I absolutely had to tell my story. When I came to the part about my son, she started looking all mournful and sad and, slowly shaking her head, leaned in true Sheryl Sandberg fashion. "But we've got to get your son back!" Was it an act? Was she sincere? One thing was certain: she had listened attentively and divined that there was an interminable sadness within me concerning Kash. That a part of me was still tender from this shitstorm of a divorce and custody battle, and she put her finger on it. And what did I do? For a moment, I really believed that "we" will work together to get my son back from my ex, even though I just met this girl that I know nothing whatsoever about.

After my mistake was gently pointed out to me, I started making excuses, like I always do: it's too expensive to wage a custody battle, the boy has already been alienated from his so-called father, my parents couldn't possibly raise two kids in their old age and so on. But isn't the real reason simply that I just don't want to put in any effort to establish a relationship with my son? I should be doing my duty as a father. I should be spending time with my son, learning about him, teaching him something, being a presence in his life, and instead I am fishing for excuses and blaming everyone and everything but myself: the circumstance, the alienation, the hurdles placed by my ex, the reciprocity my ex might seek in terms of the frequency of visitations and other real and imagined chimeras. I suppose I just don't want to do the right thing and do right by my son, if it means sacrificing my comfort and time to travel to him and get to know him. It's easy to do nothing, but is it right?

Everyone I asked had a different opinion on the matter. My dad, being most practical, counseled me to avoid forming any attachment with my son. On the face of it, it made sense: if the boy doesn't live with you, why run after him? Why get attached to someone whose life trajectory you have no influence over? He has his own life and will undoubtedly go on his own journey when he grows up. We are all just travelers after all, on this journey of life, and each person carves their own path. My mother was the exact opposite. She thought only of the child and encouraged me to do right by him. Why I took no interest in him, all the while making child support payments, was beyond her. Her father was a successful businessman and in business it is very transactional: goods and services are exchanged; when you pay for something, you have the right to expect something in return.

I wanted to delve deeper. Why? I often asked myself. Why was I so reluctant to engage with Kash? Why did I not act? Why was I paralyzed all the time? What was I afraid of? And every time I asked, all the excuses started bubbling up again. You have no time for him. You are sacrificing your time and autonomy for someone who won't appreciate you, and heck, doesn't even know you! You will have to talk to Maya again, is that what you really want? What if Maya wants to see Iris just as frequently? How will you coordinate a time and place to meet? What if you argue and it escalates, and you are hauled back to court? Why rob a child who craves your company and attention and fritter it away on someone who is really a stranger after all? What if, and this, it seemed to me, was what really gave me pause: what if I lose Iris? What if, after all my hard work, she takes to her mother, and her mother turns her against me, like she did with Kash? Some people are motivated by success; I was motivated by the fear of failure. Iris was the only person I truly loved in my life. Did I want to lose her by overplaying my hand? As I reflected on my life I realized I was adept at self-sabotage. There seemed to be a hidden internal force holding me back and I knew not what it was.

I brought this up with a girl I had started seeing who was pursuing her doctorate degree in English. We had been going out for a few months and confiding more and more to one another.

"I think I know what it is," she said. "It's not you, you see. It's your son!"

"My son?"

"He is a symbol you see. He symbolizes your greatest failure in life. Your failure as a Casanova, as a husband, and a father, yes, but also as a decent human being. You don't even have to meet him. Just thinking about him brings to mind your failed relationship with your ex, your failed attempt to disenfranchise her from all her rights, and the breakdown of any meaningful, productive or even civil discourse with her. The mere mention of his name probably calls to mind all those trips to the courtroom, the arguments advanced by the lawyers, and the loss of thousands of dollars; and, more importantly, the loss of face and of any moral high ground you ever aspired to! All those emotions rushing back into your mind probably enfeeble you to the point that you're paralyzed with fear and guilt. You fear that you will once again fail to say anything meaningful to him when you meet him, to spend time with him and only him, away from the watchful gaze of his mother. But it's perhaps a bit deeper than that. You probably fear that you've already lost him. You have lost the battle for his heart and mind, and every day you lose him more and more. Maybe one day you will reach out to him, and he won't need you anymore, and reject you like all the women that you pursued who rejected you. Who, after all, wants another failure on his hands?"

I pretended to take her seriously for a second. "Hmmm! I thought you were studying to be an English professor, not a psychologist! And what's this talk about failure and failing? Who are you to judge me anyway? I am not in your English 101 course, and I am not Hamlet nor was meant to be! I am just an attendant lord, one that will start a scene or two, deferential, glad to be of use…"

"Why did you stop? Keep going! Say it! Say that you are a bit obtuse!"

"Well duh! That's why I stopped. Who wants to admit that they are obtuse!"

Who knows how many women I have discussed this with over the years. It never fails to come up. How can you hide the existence of your kid? You can't say you just have one when in fact you have two. But then it bothers them on a visceral level. You mean the kids are separated? The horror! The horror! What kind of monster are you? I feel like saying, hey look, you don't know the whole story, okay? The woman hides her address from me, discourages me from seeing my son, actively contributes to parental alienation and so on. I want to be a good father. I want to help raise my son, but honestly, I have no bandwidth. I have a job, elderly parents to care for, a kid who needs me all the time, and besides, I waste time pursuing women like you! So no, I really don't have the time. But I also know it's wrong of me to not see my son for years on end, to play no part in his life, and to be no better than an ATM. But I cannot right these wrongs without going to court and spending thousands, and wasting the remaining years of my life, and in the process destroying my mental and physical health. Don't I count too? Am I also not a person with hopes and fears and dreams? What about me, goddammit?

Chapter Seventeen

The Heart is a Lonely Hunter

Unable or unwilling to engage with my son, frustrated by a lack of direction in life, and saddened by the realization that I would never amount to anything, I started consorting with nubile young women who thought of themselves as sugar babies. I had been using several dating apps, with almost no success, much to my consternation. I am sure all the guys just swipe right as their default, and all the girls just swipe left as theirs. What else could explain the discrepancy? Oh yeah, and another thing, they don't let you read your messages and respond to them unless you are a premium member; and even if I am premium, others are not, so it defeats the whole purpose. And I imagine the few women who accidentally stumbled across my somewhat threadbare profile got their basic information about me and moved on to greener pastures.

As I grew older, I got more and more likes from young women in their late teens and early twenties, who were almost invariably in college, and struggling to pay tuition. They wanted more than a chance to fulfill their sexual urges, and realized that seeking an older, more successful man made more sense for them. They could then dine in fancy restaurants, travel to exotic locales, and be provided for. Some of them had different tiers for different services. At the top tier, for a specified sum, they could be at your beck and call and stay with you as often as you wanted. At lower tiers, they were available for one-offs. The world's oldest profession reimagined for a newer age! And of course, there were some who were there for the thrill of it or were scam artists, asking for five dollars or ten, with vague promises of a pleasant surprise, or quite willing to meet at a restaurant, but then being no shows, or just ghosting when it suited them.

This was the culmination of a long journey. I started perusing the glossy pages of magazines when I was too young to know myself, let alone others, going on different matrimonial and dating websites and finding, much to my consternation, that the "magic" never happened! In my early twenties, almost every girl was older than me, and looking for "a real man, not a boy." Even when our ages aligned, one set of circumstances or another torpedoed the relationship. I spoke too much or not enough. I spoke English when speaking Hindi would have been better. Or I spoke English with an Indian accent. I wasn't the type she had imagined. I held grudges or burned bridges before building them. In sum, I failed to impress. And to be honest, there were times when it was hard for me to fight my primeval instincts to flee because the women were either too voluble, needy, ugly, or fat. I forced myself to tolerate them sometimes, but the disgust always surfaced, sooner or later.

It seemed impossible for me to have a romantic relationship, given my family dynamics and living situation. Had I been living by myself, secure in my privacy and with the time and resources to attend to the women, things might have been different. But sandwiched as I was between my parents and my child, or more accurately, my two children and ex, I had neither the time, nor the financial freedom, nor the mojo to nurture a relationship from the start. The walls of our house were thinner than a 17-year-old anorexic girl, and any hope of privacy was illusory. Since I couldn't speak freely in my parents' house, I avoided all dalliances, lest I be found out and interrogated at length! I can only surmise how many times I must have told women to call me during work hours, because that's when I was usually free to talk and could do so unreservedly from the safety of my car or by ducking into the stairwell; of course, no one else was free at that time. They felt free when they went home, let their hair down, say around 8:30 or 9 p.m. That's when a girl was in the mood for some entertainment, some excitement, for something fun to happen. And so I never failed to disappoint, since I was winding down from my day, preparing for the next, and on high alert for eavesdroppers. But sometimes I was just too sleepy to talk.

I know what you will say: You can't bring the party home, but you can always go to one! Yes, been there and done that. I was "Robert" at 2 a.m. once, when after leaving a nightclub I decided that the night was still young, and it was a good time to check out another brothel. Trouble was, the moral rot in that whorehouse had been made palpable somehow by the sliminess of the benches and stale smells of beer. And the place was a maze of bureaucracy, bereft of romance and spontaneity. After I was brought upstairs by a burly, misshapen sack of a man, the matron came to look me up and down, then suggested I take off all my clothes, so that the girls could feel more comfortable. I ignored her. Sitting on a long, thinly upholstered table, with cracks on the leather, reminded me of similar setups in doctor's offices and I was in no mood for a physical! The women who entered, one by one, each after several minutes, tried my patience even further, and overcome by fatigue and farts, whatever notions had brought me there evaporated, like the steamy hours of that night. I decided I had had enough and told the matron I had changed my mind and was promptly escorted out. I resolved then to never patronize these kinds of businesses again and have kept my promise to myself.

I needed a more sustainable alternative, with less risk of catching pathogens. Engaging with ladies of the night began to seem more and more like licking a public urinal, and I again surfed the rising tide of dating apps. But so many of them were riddled with bots and so many others with onlookers and thrill seekers, or worse, people bored out of their minds, who swiped right to relieve their ennui. Sometimes I felt like an ornament in a glass menagerie, a collectible on a shelf. The incredible choice afforded by these apps and the superficial nature of the interactions felt so transactional. The same forces that brought people together drove them apart, and if it was easy to meet people, it was just as easy to ghost them. I said as much to Diana on our first, and as is usually the case, last date.

Diana had a pleasant enough personality, but there was no chemistry. "Yes, that's true," she drawled in her slightly southern accent. "But you know what, dating apps are how people meet these days."

"I know. I am not a luddite. I love tech. But look around, Diana. Everywhere people are plugged in to tech and plugged out from others. I get on the subway and everyone's on their phones. I stepped out on the street the other day and almost got run over by a biker who was riding fast and looking down at his phone! I came to this cafe to meet you just now, and since I was a few minutes early, guess what? I took out my phone and started interacting with it. Even when people are with others, say in a public place, they are separated by technology. And on dating apps, you can be connected to someone, but the interface is like a wall that's keeping you apart. When we do break through that wall, like just now, we are finally meeting in person. But when we leave here, we will once again be behind our digital walls."

Diana was smiling and nodding along but I had an uneasy feeling that her eyes were glazing over. "Ah yes, speaking of which, I really should get going now, I think. It's getting late. It was nice meeting you."

With that, I paid the check, and we went our separate ways. I texted her when I reached home, saying how nice it was to meet her and wouldn't she like to get together again, but never heard back. Typical.

Chapter Eighteen

A Passage to India

Looking back on it now, I remember how it all started. How my parents would endeavor to knock some sense into me, with mixed results. And I remember how dad and mom came in one day and I could tell they were in a mood for a heart-to-heart.

Mom looked at me with a pitiful gaze. "You know we won't be around forever, my dear son."

"I know, Ma." I could feel the old, familiar lecture coming on about the importance of finding "a life partner" and dire warnings of incredibly bad stuff for those who failed in this endeavor.

"You will be left alone, in your later years, with no one to help you, care for you, and no one with whom you can share your innermost thoughts and feelings."

Dad had been pensive and distant, but now seemed to be hatching a plan. "You know, we can take out an ad in the paper, like we did some time ago, and make another trip to India!"

Mom cut in. "Yes, but she has to be educated and compatible with his personality and a nice person, not like the crazy lady we got last time. . . "

I remember "the last time." This was a few years ago, when I was still single, and had arrived in New Delhi to find a wife.

Traveling such distances got you a sore back, constipation and a fuzzy head, especially on non-stop flights from Newark. One got the feeling of having aged considerably in the span of a few hours: joints ached and cracked; muscles went stiff; throats got dry and raspy; and eyes, heavy with sleep, struggled to see out from drooping eyelids. After the flight's indignities--the stale air, the leftovers served at mealtimes, the cramped seats and restrooms, and the bright fluorescent lights and interminable hum of the engines, one finally landed, only to then fill out customs forms, stand in more lines, be interrogated by strangers, and to find a way out of the bloody airport. And yet, that is but the beginning. The beginning of a slow, agonizing car ride to your destination, as it snakes, worm-like, through the clogged arteries of New Delhi, with everyone honking their horn and driving how they please. And God help you if you go directly to meet your relatives, as we often did, for further interrogation and inspection. Sometimes I felt I would throw up and pass out at the sight of more food and small talk, when what I really wanted was to take a dump, a hot shower, and then hit the sack.

Of course, you would wake up at odd hours of the night the first few nights, so that during the day, in bright sunlight, you *felt* that it was the dead of night somewhere else in the world. The Sheraton we stayed at was decent. Large, airy lobby, ornate chandeliers, well-appointed guest rooms, a complimentary, full-service breakfast every morning, and lush gardens and grounds made up for one's travails on the journey here. But it was the human element that excited me! Young, beautiful girls from all over the country came to meet us at the hotel lobby; and as we drank tea and munched on tasty samosas, we would put the questions to them and their families and watch them smugly as they twisted and contorted themselves and visibly squirmed in their seats. Dad's favorite question was always, "Where do you see yourself in five years?" Mom's concerns were more culinary, and mine more practical: did we have enough in common to build a life together or would we be two strangers trapped in a prison of our own making? At the debrief, dad would share his reservations about a particular candidate: "You see," he would say, "she was more interested in having a full-fledged career than starting a family in five years. Shows us that she is not a family-oriented homemaker."

I liked the sumptuous breakfast at the hotel. We sat at an elegant table and were served by young men who were deadly serious about their jobs, as evidenced by their impeccably ironed uniforms. You ate what you wanted to your heart's content: pooris, dosas, sambar, sandwiches, and new delicacies we had never tried before. Then the day would begin. Sometimes we would interview candidates right at the hotel, and sometimes be chauffeured across the city or to other cities to meet prospective candidates.

Every time we visited New Delhi we always spent the better half of the day with my dad's older brother. He was in his late eighties, gaunt, frail, and wholly dependent on his two sons and on the household help hired for his massages and mobility. His wife was around the same age as him but blind in one eye and almost blind in the other. My older cousin, Pankaj, was short and stout, and had a bit of a beer belly, though he never drank to excess. While he could reliably be counted on to crow about his U.N. job whenever the opportunity presented itself, and never failed to mention how he was exempt from paying taxes, his trophy wife, Nandini, was his opposite: humble, unpretentious, and helpful. The younger cousin, Niraj, was bald, even in his twenties, and so it took him forever to attract a mate. On more than one occasion I heard him say, "It's just a mental block," when nagged about his hairless head and how it was ruining his love life. Being just a chartered accountant, his job was much less glamorous than his older brother's and so he kept a low profile most of the time.

Somehow, I felt cheated by my cousins. They had both grown up in India, in their native soil, and soaked up the nuances and intricacies of the dominant Hindu culture, whereas I had been transplanted to an alien nation. Perhaps the acidity and vitriol of my adopted soil, coupled with a healthy penchant for xenophobia, molded me subtly to identify as neither Indian nor American. America othered me and my native land disowned me. I was simply insufficiently Indian: I neither watched nor enjoyed Hindi movies and music, had no friends of Indian descent, socialized with no one outside work, and so had no conception of myself as a part of something larger. I just didn't belong! And quite frankly, I didn't belong because I didn't want to belong. In the heyday of my youth I saw myself as better than everyone else and felt no pressing need to change this conception of myself as I grew older.

It's remarkable how things pan out or they don't. When I was in college I poured all my energy and time into my major. I memorized poetry, wrote short stories and essays, and read canonical works. I wanted to be the best, to pursue knowledge and excellence, to be "the paragon of all animals" as they say. But when I finally started to apply to jobs, and read the job descriptions and requirements, I realized nobody had any use for an English major. So all that applying, all that work, all that struggle, for what? Throughout high school and college I walked the straight and narrow and told myself that this was the way to success, and yet, right before I graduated college, a professor told me that there was something keeping me from success--a hidden force, almost, that made for self-sabotage and kept me from achieving my dreams. But what were my dreams? Did I ever really want to become someone or was I just living someone else's life? When I entered the world of work, I was conscientious and diligent, attending classes at night and working weekends as a matter of course; putting in late hours in offices from New York to Philadelphia and Birmingham. Instead of attending mixers and parties in my youth, I applied myself and continually spread myself thin, like butter on bread, and just as the bread soaks the butter so it's no longer visible, the days of my life were soaked up in constant toil and abnegation. I arrived in America during my formative years, and through dint of hard work and perseverance, coupled with parental support, I think I turned out okay in the end. Yet success in professional ventures does not always lead to success in personal life, and I could never find a true friend or female companionship.

Chapter Nineteen

It All Goes to Pot

"So, tell me about New York," demanded Pankaj as soon as he saw us entering through the arched doorway of his house.

"What would you like to know?"

His eyes lit up and he chuckled softly. "I want to know if you guys are still picking up after your dogs!"

"Yes, of course! It's the law in New York! But *we* don't do that since we don't *have* a dog!"

And then we both had a nice belly laugh. It was our inside running joke for many years. I had told both my cousins once how people needed to pick up after their dogs and they were so incredulous they couldn't stop laughing. At that moment both swore they would never live in the U.S.

After tea, cake, and some pleasantries, the conversation took a more serious turn. Pankaj surprised dad and mom by declaring that he had placed an ad in the local papers for a bride without telling us, and now, lo and behold, we had quite a few girls and their families interested. These were mostly names and phone numbers listed on 3 by 5 memo book pages. I felt better now because there was something concrete to go on. The soft, silken texture of these slips of paper held vast potential and promise. Of course, I pretended to be cavalier about it, and handed it back to dad after a cursory look.

We had rented a two-bedroom apartment in New Delhi, at a discounted rate, courtesy of some of the perks available to former Indian Air Force officers like my dad. After we got there and showered, I just crashed on the hard, narrow bed and lost consciousness. I came to after a few hours in a confused state. There were red bumps on my legs and feet, and they itched terribly. I thought I had turned on the fan to keep the mosquitoes away, but the fan was off, and I was covered in sweat. I got up slowly and toggled the light switches on and off. Nothing. And then it hit me: there had been a power outage. It was a common phenomenon in New Delhi, and I was accustomed to it when I lived here as a child, but had since forgotten.

It was the middle of the afternoon, but it felt more like 7 a.m. We were leaving for a village on the outskirts of Punjab in a few minutes. But first we had to stop in town to meet up with a promising prospect: an innocent-looking young woman, named Bhumika, with a disarming smile and a cheerful disposition. But what's an adventure without an obstacle course? The girl lived with her parents in a dilapidated part of town, with narrow dirt alleys leading up to the front door. And having nothing better to do, one or two cows and a few dogs had decided to camp out in the hot sun and people-watch. As I navigated gingerly around one cow, then another, careful to avoid the latter's protruding horns, I felt the stare of multitudes leaning over their balconies, scrutinizing and perhaps snickering to see a tyro in these parts. The home was simple enough, and the girl was pretty. She looked no older than a teenager, in fact. We talked but couldn't really talk freely in front of company. It was more genial small talk and certain courtesies and niceties. So much of our existence is frittered away in these small, inconsequential moments. Things were generally going well, but I had some minor reservations.

I caught my sister looking askance at me when we got in the car to leave. "So, what do you think?" she asked.

"Well, she is nice and all, but she does have a little bit of a stomach." I said.

"Stomach!" she snorted. "Well, so do you!"

"You know what I mean."

"That's a baby bump. It's part of her uterus."

"Whatever. Let's not talk about it."

"Can't believe you will disqualify someone, based just on that. How superficial of you!"

"It's not just that. It's a long road. She is still studying, so when will she be done, when will she be ready?"

Dad had been enjoying the exchange. He piped up now. "What's the rush?"

"No rush dad, let's all just go back home," I said.

"Stop it, you two," said mom impatiently.

Dad had begun to squirm in his seat. "Speaking of stopping, we need to make a pit stop, people. I have to use the facilities."

Now, it was the driver's turn to contribute his two cents. *"Jaam laga hai sahib!"* he mumbled and pointed toward the traffic jam.

Dad leaned over the side of the car and folded the side view mirror. "That's why it's taking so long, you moron! Now, drive like you live here for God's sake. Look, there's a big store. I bet they have a toilet."

Sitting in the car with the AC running was slightly better than sitting in the sauna. We were still melting like candles, with sweat beads running down our temples. Dad took what seemed like an inordinate amount of time in the restroom. When he finally returned, he looked at me sheepishly and smiled faintly. He said nothing and I thought I saw a look of resignation darken his visage. The driver was unsure of the way, and I flagged down a rusty old farmer dressed in his white kurta and dhoti and asked for directions. He looked a little baffled by my Punjabi accent, but my mom was impressed that I had coaxed even that much language out of myself.

If you thought the potholes were bad in New York, you were blissfully ignorant. After a while, potholes and gashes were all that remained, with narrow dirt roads appearing more and more frequently. By the time we arrived at our destination, our bones had been rattled and shaken, and the color drained out of our cheeks. The town had a bustling market square and a big sculpture of Lord Hanuman at the center. The driver stopped at an imposing house, with a muddy front porch and two concrete pillars denoting the entrance.

This particular specimen was fair with comely features, and a smidge taller than me. I was underwhelmed. Yes, she would be a good match for me, but why should I be nervous? Here she was in a one-horse town, the roads around riddled with potholes and the people ignorant and poor, while I was the glittering Prince Charming from America. She needed rescuing more than me! So I sat down with an air of authority and coolly looked around the room. As I did so I thought I saw her mother's gaze fixed intently on me.

Whenever I would look at her mother, she would look away, pretending to scrutinize the little paintings and photos around her house. After eating the poori aloo lunch of fried golden-brown pancakes and spiced potatoes and after sipping the homemade tea, dad began gingerly broaching the subject of marriage. He only needed to say, "So, how do you think we should proceed" to change the tenor in the room and draw a look of consternation in her mother's face. And the more he spoke about my particulars and the suitability of the match, the more somber the parents' visages grew. After some time the wife motioned to the husband and the two excused themselves for a few minutes.

When they emerged from behind closed doors a different energy animated them, and they spoke quietly and firmly. Being in the other room I could not make out the words, but the import was to tactfully decline the marriage proposal. My two cousins seemed to take offense and started haggling aggressively as if they were in a fish market, but that only cemented the parents' resolve.

The ride back was quiet and quite bumpy, as we all processed what had just transpired. It's somewhat akin, I suppose, to politicians who never bother writing a concession speech, figuring they couldn't possibly lose. The somber mood trailed us all the way back to dad's ancestral home in Ludhiana, where we were staying for the night. My cousins had attempted to lighten the mood several times in the car by, of all things, comparing water bottles purchased at roadside stores along the way, remarking on the authenticity of the label on the bottle, and inferring which product was spring water and which was merely tap. But the elephant on the roof of the car was never acknowledged, and so their efforts fell flat.

After reaching home and noshing on dal and roti, the conversation once again centered around the epic fail today, mainly because grandpa was a curious man and wanted all the details.

"I still don't understand why they said no!" he shouted in frustration after listening to the events of the day.

The room was silent. My gaze was transfixed on the neatly patterned tiles made by the bricks in the yard. Their clear symmetry had a somewhat hypnotizing effect.

"What is it?" he continued. "Don't they want our good family name? Is there anything wrong with this handsome young man?" and glared at me.

"He is getting to be almost thirty years old," grandma said ruefully.

Raju was getting visibly agitated. "Ah, stop this nonsense, I say! We have so many other candidates, pages full of them from all over the–"

"But mostly in New Delhi!" interjected Sonu.

Mom almost leapt up with joy. "That's right! Good boy!" She went over to dad and placed her hand on his shoulder. "Isn't that right, Koko? Don't you have all those sheets filled with details of the girls that came in from the newspaper?"

Dad took a furtive glance at me and squirmed uneasily. "Well, not exactly–"

Grandpa had been stewing for some time but now it seemed he had had enough. "Forget New Delhi! Girls there are fast and loose. No morals, family values, heck no family even sometimes. Running around naked on the streets like harlots! If the boy is well-qualified and a good provider, they will come running, believe me. When I first got started, I earned only seventeen rupees monthly and was able to employ two servants on that income. I had a bicycle and a healthy bank account. I can't imagine he earns much on his teacher's salary, though."

"I hate to break up the party, but I think I will call it a night. It's been a long day." And with that, I walked out of the room, disgusted with all the talk and fuss over my prospects for marriage or the lack thereof. As I was walking back from the restroom after brushing my teeth I heard some whispers in the dark and stayed a while to eavesdrop. It was my cousins Sonu and Raju, sharing their insights about me.

"It's not just that, yaar," continued Sonu, "he doesn't even stand up straight when he walks. No girl wants to marry a hunchback."

Raju cleared his throat. "And you notice how he is always picking his nose, especially when he thinks no one's watching?"

"That, and he is already going bald. Not a good look, if you ask me."

"Neeraj is bald too, Sonu, but at least he has a good job. Who wants to marry a schoolteacher? Not exactly a prestigious profession, you know?"

And with that I slithered away and lay down on the charpai. It was a warm summer night, and I wanted to look up at the stars in silence. But the stars looked blurry through my misty eyes and by and by they grew heavy with sleep.

Chapter Twenty

A Very Short Engagement

It seems mom had again pressed dad in the middle of the night to contact the girls in New Delhi and in the morning he had an announcement to make.

"Good morning, everyone," he began as we were drinking our tea. "Yesterday was a long, hard day of travel, as you know. But unfortunately in some ways it was even harder for *me*." He paused. "Yes, for me. You see, when we had stopped for our rest stop along the way the facilities were inadequate, or rather, undersupplied."

The blank looks around the room flustered him. "What I am trying to say is that I had to use the toilet and there was no toilet paper, so I was forced to wipe my ass with the matrimonial prospects."

A pause ensued as everyone digested this new development. Grandpa smiled contemptuously, as if to say he didn't expect much more from his son; grandma was her usual downcast and sorrowful self; Sonu was still half-asleep and Raju tittered nervously, while mom was simply lost in the museum of Modern Art, scrutinizing a Kandinsky piece.

Dad came over to me and touched my shoulder. "Sorry son," he said lugubriously, and ambled to the latrine in the far corner of the open compound. No reason for anyone else to stay and look embarrassed or sorry for me when the main character himself bows out, and so they all left, ostensibly to take care of their own urgent affairs. "How everything turns away quite leisurely from the disaster," I muttered, and left the room in disgust.

Later that afternoon, mom came over, with a glitter in her eyes and a dreamy excitement in her voice, so that for a minute I was deeply suspicious and felt as though I were being mocked.

"Good news, *beta*," she began. "Your uncle has identified a promising young girl not too far from here. We are all going over in the evening!"

"That's great! Have fun!" I snapped.

"C'mon, *beta*! Dad didn't mean it. You know it was an emergency." She hesitated, then, "I am sure you would have done the same if you were in his place."

I gave her a sidelong glance but assented to her request. I had grown sympathetic to their cause, which is a strange thing to say I guess, since their cause was really my own, and in theory I shouldn't have needed any persuading.

Fortunately, this prospect was much closer than the last. The roads were potholed and muddy as usual, especially since it had rained of late. But getting there was much less painful. The girl's name was Jessica, and I remember this because I ended up getting engaged to her the next day. It's a tragicomedy what a man's hormones, combined with circumstances beyond his control, will make him do.

Halfway through the samosas and the tea, just as the conversation got going, the lights went out. There was something magical about the evening, as we lounged by candlelight, the moths flitting around us and then hissing on their kamikaze missions into the flames.

In the absence of serious misgivings or incompatibility, the Indian psyche usually defaults to a yes when it comes to matrimony. I once read somewhere that the Chinese always look for doors of equal sizes to gauge compatibility when it comes to relationships. Most of the time we do something similar when we meet with one another's families, for as the saying goes, "The apple doesn't fall far from the tree." A marriage can never just be between two people, since they were not in a cocoon their entire lives. We are the sum of our experiences, the product of our times, and are shaped by all we have met.

I suppose part of it also had to do with my own mental state and unfulfilled desires. There's a pretty girl at work, Nicole, and to gaze at her is solace enough, but sometimes I am smitten with her and work becomes impossible. I keep thinking, how can I get with this woman? God, what would it feel like to possess her completely, to squeeze her breasts in my hands, to have her writhe and moan, our limbs entwined, our flesh merged into one flesh. It would be nirvana surely, an incredible feeling of ecstasy and oblivion. But alas! That shall never be in this lifetime, for she is so much younger than me, calls me a weirdo for not drinking, and I am sure sees the bald spot in the middle of my hair and snickers. I must pine away for her alone while making do with the hand that's dealt to me. Indeed, my right hand must suffice if I cannot have her! And so I agreed to my second engagement to Jessica, and to once again suffer the intricate rituals of the ceremony, the parade of ladoos, and of people who came to shake my hand and slap me on the shoulder.

But a second engagement is just that: a second engagement. Been there, done that! A few years ago, before my herniated discs and sciatica, there was the original article: my engagement to Garvita. Our family came to know about Garvita through my sister, Meena. Meena had attended Nyenrode University in The Netherlands and had earned her MBA after the death of her first husband. Someone there informed us that a single girl was looking to get hitched and also completing her MBA at the same university. She was staying at her uncle's and had family back home in India. Her uncle and aunt were eager beavers and after some preliminaries decided to swoop down into JFK. Given that Garvita was a few inches taller than me, a few days before their arrival my parents decided to take me shopping at Macys for high-heeled shoes. After that, dad constantly chided me for my poor posture and commanded me to stand erect, since he had been in the Indian Air Force and thus knew all about military discipline. Finally, the day arrived. We took two cars to the airport. On the ride home, Meena arranged it so that Garvita and I rode by ourselves. After twenty minutes we stopped for gas and Meena came over and asked if we were interested in one another. It would have been quite embarrassing to say no, so I just politely nodded in agreement, without knowing much about her.

The next day we went shopping for a diamond ring, and the day after that was the hastily arranged and rather rushed engagement. There was the usual dancing, music, pictures and the handful of guests cobbled together through brief phone calls and pithy emails.

And just like that, the next afternoon at 5 p.m. this bird is on the wing and back in Amsterdam. We communicate continuously and incessantly, via emails, texts, calls. It gets so much we run out of things to say. So being in our twenties we start dabbling in sexual fantasies and give voice to our repressed desires. We conspire to do the deed when I visit her in a few days. But what pretext should we use? Yes, I know, she says, let's tell them we are going to a party at the university and then we'll sneak off. I will take you to my room and we will be alone together.

And so, I could barely contain my excitement and told my folks and my sister about this incredible party happening at the university and that I was invited. Well, that was it! First Meena flew into a rage and then seethed internally. How dare she invite you and not me? Dad and mom tried to placate her by saying it must have been an oversight on her part; I tried to laugh it off, but to no avail. She had it in for that girl and was bent on destroying my relationship with her. Tickets were booked in a huff, and my folks urged me to go with Meena to Amsterdam and support her in this endeavor. Blood is thicker than water, they said; we are family, we must stick together. We brought this woman into your life and have now determined she is unfit for our family. Goaded by these exhortations I went foolishly, compelled by a will not my own, and by a force unseen. I sat in the living room of Garvita's uncle's house and sided with my sister and participated in the discord that followed. The narrow streets in their suburb were dotted with horse dung and a faint mist and drizzle kept us company.   As we were driving back to the airport, suddenly the sun came out and we had to shield our eyes with the visor in the car. It was 10:30 p.m. After this trip, for many days and nights, I was but the shell of a man. Simply going through the motions of quotidian life. I was working for a consulting firm at the time and stuck in Birmingham for most of the week at the client site. Life had ceased to be purposeful, so one day I sneezed carelessly, and something snapped in my body. I ended up with two herniated discs. Just the thing to compound the emotional pain!

Chapter Twenty-One

Soni's Blues

After my engagement to Jessica, there was nothing to do but fly back home and wonder how I had once again narrowly avoided diabetes. The parade of ladoos and the multiple boxes of sweets were cloying to the point of inducing PTSD. We didn't really talk all that much, and then almost infrequently, as the days went by. I considered myself a romantic, but not overly sentimental, and so I knew that since both our families were traditionally Indian, our conversations would likely not remain private. And since we were not in love, I simply kept to myself; in fact, our families had more interaction than us.

Jessica's dad was engaged in his daughter's life and wanted a play-by-play of my progress in acquiring U.S. citizenship. But that goal seemed elusive to me back then. There was an anti-immigrant fervor at that time, with deportations, hate crimes, and outright hostility and xenophobia; and almost every day was marked by churn and social upheaval. Against this backdrop, the questions from Jessica's father pestering me about my citizenship status arrived with alarming predictability. I wondered why these people could not keep up with the news, for surely they would then have seen the disconnect between the current political reality and their expectations. And yet, had it stopped there, we still might have salvaged something. But mom began intricate discussions with Jessica's mother on the details of the wedding, the jewelry, the fashion choices made by Jessica, the mores in the U.S., and her plans for her future daughter-in-law and the daughter-in-law's expectations of her life with her mother-in-law. I always say leave it to the women to chop each other's heads off! It never fails. So, unsurprisingly, things didn't quite pan out in the end.

As the years dragged on, the days and weeks blended seamlessly into an infinite, interminable loop of work and leisure. Lacking any real friends, meaningful hobbies, passions, or pursuits, I found plenty of time for reflection and self-doubt. My mind traced an arc connecting my multiple engagements and their unraveling, and I saw that while some events were beyond my influence, in others I had played the principal part. Somewhere in that tangled web of associations and dissociations my relationship with Bhumika also unraveled, chipped away bit by bit by time and circumstance. It wasn't a formal engagement this time but a verbal assurance from her parents that our relationship was a done deal. But the reality was that they were just biding their time until either the father got a job in the U.S., or the daughter was able to secure a student visa to study abroad. The promise of marriage was a façade–all part of a contingency plan in case nothing materialized for the family. Well, guess what? Something did! Bhumika was accepted into a Canadian university, and we were told to wait some more while she finished her studies and found a suitable job. Obviously, that was not tenable.

Despite these setbacks, I was not one to quit so easily. I kept running after women long past my prime, sometimes using subterfuge and outright lies and misrepresentations to grasp at a chance to be appraised by them, like an ornament in a china shop, beneath the bright hot lights of judgment.

A few years after my divorce, I was mindlessly browsing profiles of women on some Indian matrimonial website. One, Soni, stood out among all others: not because she was ravishingly beautiful, but because she was easy to talk to and accomplished in myriad other ways: she had her doctorate from the U.S., and was employed as a professor in the field of sociology. But those were mundane details. What interested me was that I could finally have a real conversation with her. We could discuss anything and everything. This deep emotional, intellectual, and psychological connection, however, was undercut by her appearance. She had a protruding jaw, with a set of teeth like miniature chessmen and multiple spots and blotches sprinkled throughout her brown face. I again felt judged by the eyes of other women who passed us by on the sidewalk. It was almost as if they all seemed to say, "C'mon, you can do better than her!" and "Really, that's who you chose to be with?!" and "Surely, you jest!" I fancied hearing such judgments from all who crossed our path and felt tortured by these voices!

Nevertheless, given how much we had in common, we kept meeting and talking, and one day I even drove to her house and slept with her. In time our connection deepened and as it did she expected more and more from me, and merely talking on the phone, while it suited me just perfectly, was simply not enough for her. Even after she took a job in North Carolina, we kept talking for hours and hours for days on end. I took the initiative to book a flight to see her on her birthday. But then I canceled this flight when we had a slight argument. Days later, we made up and I regretted my actions. So, I booked another flight and felt much happiness. It was short-lived. The next day I again canceled my ticket. It wasn't the money: whether the airline would refund the fare or not made not that much of a difference. They said they would, and that was a bit of a comfort, but the larger issue was this: I asked myself whether I really liked this woman to be with her for 48 hours. The answer was an unequivocal no, and I couldn't bring myself to take the trip after all. With every passing day, the knowledge that I would eventually have to spend two entire days and nights with her began to gnaw at me, made me anxious and nervous beyond all reason, and terrified me when I imagined all the possible ways in which this rendezvous could go wrong.

Suddenly I had an epiphany: why was I taking this trip if I genuinely wasn't attracted to this woman? Sure, I enjoyed talking to her, listening to the sound of her voice, her ideas appealed to me, we made each other laugh, and we had a great time together. All of that was indubitably true but I was never sexually attracted to her, and as much as I wanted her only as a friend, she wanted me as a lover and a partner. Now, if I were attracted intellectually, physically, and sexually to a woman and she consistently denied me sex, why would I continue to pursue her? If my love and affection were not reciprocated, then why persist? So, really, I could not blame her for being upset with me.

Upon reflection, I couldn't believe I had changed so much in such a short period of time. For most of my life I did everything in my power, at every stage of my life, just to get laid! From consorting with sex workers to deceiving women left and right, to several one-night stands. The list goes on. For years on end, through good times and bad, I stuck with it: driving, flying, stumbling, running long distances for carnal pleasure. And now, when it is right in front of me, when the lady is essentially spreading her knees, and effectively supplicating me to possess her completely, I demur! That is just so not like me! And yet, as I tell myself repeatedly, at the risk of sounding like a tuneless trombone, I long not for the sex, but rather mourn the loss of a beautiful friendship. Oh, how I connected with this woman intellectually and spiritually! How many truly transcendent moments we shared together, when we escaped the grim, sad reality of our banal lives and were transported to a state of intellectual bliss; two academics arguing about nothing in particular. Alas!

A week after canceling my ticket, I called her. Of course, she didn't pick up the phone. I then texted her, "Can we talk," and after some time she texted back, "What is there to talk about?" So I called again and this time she picked up.

I tried to keep it cool and casual.

"How are you, Soni?"

"Fine, Ajay, and you?"

"Good. Are you mad at me?

"No. I understand why you did it."

"Do you, really? I don't think I understood why for a few days, and in fact I wrestled with myself for a week before mustering the courage to call you. I was so ashamed and embarrassed and angry at myself that I just couldn't talk to you before."

"Okay, so what do you want now? You flip flop so much; do you even know what you want?"

"I know what I want, and that's why I am calling. I am calling because I think we have so much going for us on so many fronts but one. We connect spiritually, mentally, we laugh together, we–"

"Stop it, Ajay. This is BS. I know all this, but so what? I can't just be friends with you after we have been intimate. Do you know–?"

"I know, I know, just hear me out. Why throw away everything after we built it up for six months? We put so much time and effort into this relationship…"

"And what came of it, huh? You just unilaterally decided to cancel your ticket without even consulting me? Where is the partnership in that? Where is the respect in that? I deserved better than that strange and insulting text you sent me that morning."

"I didn't send any insulting text to you. I even apologized in that text, saying I hope you can forgive me."

"What a big favor you did for me, eh? I am supposed to be so grateful to you for that."

"Listen, all I am saying is, I mean, if I can just say one thing to you, it is this: I really like you as a friend, and I have no other friends, and I really hope we can continue to talk and maybe even meet as friends. For me, it's just hard to go from zero to sixty, like you do in a car. You know, since we don't have any interaction on a regular basis in person, just the thought of spending two days and nights with you, it was a bit much for me. But hey, if you don't want to be friends with me, I will understand. I would probably do the same thing as you are doing now, but at least I now have a clear conscience–I can say that it wasn't me who ended the relationship–it was you."

"Oh! How convenient, Ajay. When it suits you, you can just end the relationship all by yourself, and when it suits you, you come crawling back and try to make me feel guilty for ending it!"

"No, no, I am not trying to make you feel guilty. I am apologizing for my actions, and honestly I don't know what came over me. I mean, I think of myself as a very rational and logical guy, and so I was really shocked that I did what I did."

"So be logical and rational Ajay, and find someone local, who you can see every day. Okay? Bye now."

"Okay, then, bye."

I felt better after this conversation. It was something off my chest. Yes, I was at fault. Yes, I don't know why I did this or why I bothered calling her after I sort of figured out why I did this, but at least I didn't end it myself, at least I tried to be friends with her. But again, she doesn't want a friend. She wants a lover. And so, literally, I couldn't be the man she wanted me to be. Even though I have no body image issues or deformities, in her eyes I just didn't measure up, if you will excuse the pun.

As usual, I told all this to Neal, and he was unconvinced.

"I don't know man; I think there has to be something deeper than this to it. Don't you think?"

"Maybe, there is, Neal," I said. "Come to think of it, there sure is. I mean, the lady doesn't just want to be friends. She has made that loud and clear to me. I think what she really wants is control–"

"Yeah, now we're talking," he interjected. "Like they say in our line of work, root cause analysis, man. What is the root cause for all this, I don't know, emotional mess?"

"Mess it is, my friend, and boy, what a mess! Like I was saying, it's almost like she processes it differently. She wants a full-fledged, no-holds-barred, above-board relationship, where she can tell her friends and colleagues at her college that I am her "partner" and introduce me to her sisters. And all that is fine with me, if she wants to do that, but it doesn't end there. She wants me to return the favor and tell my parents and family that I am in a relationship with her, with all the attendant meaning that term implies: that it is an emotional and physical relationship. I can't do that, and she doesn't understand it."

"You know, she might hold a grudge, Ajay. She might blame you for it if–"

"She does, Neal!" I cried. "She sure does! You put your finger on it. She finds ways to tell me that she loves me, but I don't love her back or don't love her in the same way. She will find ways to insinuate that I am a bad person, to guilt-trip me into doing or saying something, or to do emotional blackmail. Heck, it reminds me of my ex-wife. Like, for instance, she will say, 'I love you,' and then there will be a long and uncomfortable pause. It's almost comical in a way, because she expects me to say, 'I love you' back but I just can't. I mean, I don't love her. Should I just lie about it? And then, there are instances when she will forcibly do something when she doesn't get her way. Once when we were having sex she said, 'Come all the way in, all the way in,' and I said, 'I am all the way in,' and she acted all frustrated and grabbed my buttocks and thrust me even deeper inside her. To be honest, that hurt a bit because my foreskin was already stretched to the max, and then she had to suddenly strain it even further without warning!"

Neal was doubled up with laughter now and I just walked away. What kind of person takes pleasure in someone's pain like that?

Gradually, the realization dawned upon me that it was perhaps fruitless to even pursue women, given my current family situation and constraints. Even if a woman were to overlook all my faults and accept me for who I am, I still could not commit wholeheartedly to her. Maybe I would if she were truly attractive, but why would a truly attractive woman want to be with me? What would be her incentive? Worse still, perhaps her only incentive would be something extraneous: a desire to better her situation (like the woman from New Delhi who just wanted to use me to escape the pollution in her town) and let slip this sentiment quite by accident one day! Or like my ex, who just wanted a green card and a payday.

What does a dog do after it finally catches the car? For years, I prayed to God to once again give me a woman I could cuddle up with in the dark, our limbs entwined in the lonely hours of the night, breathing softly in unison as we slept. And lo! He answered my prayers! After so many years of longing for something and then finally attaining it, I no longer cared for it. And so I was sad for many days after this fiasco of a relationship that crashed and burned like a Cessna.

The sun beat down relentlessly on the white, hot pavement in the waning days of summer and for my last few vacation days I closeted myself to store the grief of my accumulated years. Having invested so much emotional energy, innumerable hours conversing on the phone, sharing stories, joys, fears and philosophies, to have it come to an abrupt and silent end suddenly heightened the morbidity and monotony of life.

Chapter Twenty-Two

A Noiseless Patient Spider

Time marched on and I felt myself drifting. What difference had my life made for anyone? Lying on my deathbed I would be tinged with regret; not necessarily for all the things I had not accomplished, or the places I had not visited, but for that one person I could have helped but chose not to. I had brought him into this world, didn't I owe him something? Why was I neglecting him? His thoughts clouded my judgment and sapped my strength. Everything I did was tinged with a longing for him. And so, once again, I endeavored to be a better person. I fired off emails to my nemesis and asked for an audience with my son. At first she made every excuse imaginable: he is busy, he has allergies, he is recovering from surgery, and then how she is working weekends, and he is in school on weekdays so no visitation would be possible. When I pressed her on it and made it clear that I was determined to see him, she reluctantly agreed to take off on a Sunday, a month and a half in the future.

As I waited for the appointed day, I gamed out all the different scenarios in my head. What would I say and how would I say it? Surely, I would have a Herculean task convincing him to come with me, since he would have been coached and brainwashed into not complying. I bought all kinds of gifts for him, a mix of tchotchkes and electronics, and packed and repacked everything, considering what would appeal to him and what he might find frivolous. That morning I informed my parents that I was going to the city to see my son. As usual, dad was indifferent, but mom was curious. She floated the idea of coming along, and I agreed, figuring this may be the last time she sees Kash, given her advanced age and myriad health issues. I finished all my errands on Saturday and off we went on Sunday to the city of fragile dreams, also known as Manhattan. Of course, we had plenty of company along the way. It was a sunny Sunday afternoon, the cerulean sky punched with puffy white clouds, and no one wanted to be home.

I remember how long it took to get there, after traversing the Brooklyn Queens Expressway, then making our way to Battery Park City and circling the blocks looking for a parking spot. Finding street parking saved us a few dollars and we were grateful. First we located a Shake Shack and used the facilities. Then we went by the water to sample the salt air hoping for a breeze on this hot day. Almost all the benches were being used but one and we sat in the blinding sun, watching the people amble, bike, and rollerblade past us. As it was almost time for the visitation, another visit to the restroom was warranted. When we emerged again into the bright sunshine, I called to inquire about the meeting and was curtly directed to come inside the playground.

Suddenly, I spotted the pair that had made my life wretched and miserable. The woman was nearly as obese as I expected, but the boy had grown taller and had a fair complexion. They were waiting patiently under a tree, next to hordes of screaming children running around the playground. A plot was afoot, and it was written plainly on their faces. Kash had been coached to resist my entreaties to spend any time alone with me, or even talk to me, and when I decided to stand there and wait to see how things would pan out, Maya motioned to him to run along and he did so with much haste, as if his life depended upon making an escape.

Mother had been watching this exchange from afar and now decided to enter the playground to get closer to the action. Maya glanced at her and flipped at once.

"You said you were coming here alone, didn't you?"

"No," I said, suddenly taken aback, "I said this was my time with Kash. And besides, what is it to you who comes with me and who doesn't? She is my mother, and she can come if she wants."

"Absolutely not," she fumed. "This visitation is over." She gestured at my mother. "You know I don't get along with her."

Mom was never one to be outdone. "Get along? Who wants to get along with you? Do you think we came all this way to get along with you or see Kash?"

"That's it, Kash, let's go!" And with that she grabbed him by the arm and huffed her way out of the playground."

"What about grandparents' rights!" I shouted after her, probably against my better judgment.

So there was nothing to do but go back home. I cursed Maya and told my mother I told her this would end badly, that there was no use in reaching out to the boy. And how in the world could I convince that toxic woman I was no longer the man who had abandoned her in that New Delhi hotel? That was never me to begin with and I had evolved since! I endeavored every day to live my life simply and ethically, to be kind and patient, and to treat people with dignity and respect. I liked to believe there was no trace of that malevolence in me that had temporarily possessed my soul and poisoned my mind. Even if I could tell her somehow, why would she believe me?

I once again tried to persuade myself that we are all on our own journey in this life and sooner or later we will all come to the same unceremonious end. If this is something I cannot change, I should recognize that and act accordingly. Even if I could change it, what pyrrhic victory would that be, and at what emotional, financial and logistical cost? I must pay either way: either child support payments or payments to lawyers, the court system, and emotional bloodletting after trench warfare with my ex. It seemed like nothing mattered: no associations, no friendships, no relationships, no random acts of kindness or cruelty. Look at Ozymandias, or Caesar, or Alexander the Great! Whether a man reaches the pinnacle of achievement or drowns in the slough of despond, the result is still the same. So why the struggle, the hustle, the emotional turmoil and the desire to strive for something, anything?

And then, a bolt from the blue! A few years later, when Iris had just turned fourteen, the wench called her on her birthday, as was her custom, and this time she really took pains to start up a conversation with her. First, she tried videoconferencing me but this being so sudden and such an intrusion of my privacy, I did not pick up her phone. Instead, I made an audio call, and right away Kash came on very strong and started all these phatic, filler questions about how everything is going and how Iris' summer is shaping up and so forth. The next day, just as Iris and I were thinking we were done for another year, Maya emails to say that she would like to talk to Iris every week, at least once a week. What a shock to the system! Who wants to dredge up this old sludge and muck about in it again after so many years? Will I ever be rid of this woman, I wondered. Now that I had lost all interest in my boy, she probably perceived that and started going after Iris. So she called and wanted to step in the same river twice, or maybe to recreate what never existed in the first place. This time I indulged them and we had our video conference. I had some questions prepared for Kash, such as what he was doing over the summer and so forth, but apparently he had been coached to be evasive and gave perfunctory responses and sometimes just lied outright. For instance, when I asked about his health, he said it was "good," and when I confronted him with his hospital stay for two days, he said he "could not remember" why he went to the hospital, looking with shifty eyes at his mother, who was just off-camera for clues on how to respond. I felt like a fake asking him anything, because after so many years he was just a stranger to me. He peppered Iris with questions about her likes and dislikes and hobbies and so forth, but all that felt pointless and futile. I felt I had no moral authority over this boy, and that even if he were to visit me and stay with me, I would be greatly inconvenienced, since he would effectively be just a spy for his mother and his real family back home. Did I want to feel insecure in my own house with his presence? So no, it would never do to invite him here; and moreover, why did I even bother making conversation with him? What would that accomplish?

To reckon with the emotional pain of these series of failed relationships, at first I brought more blight on myself: actively seeking out and consorting with total strangers, talking for hours with prospects I met at "matrimonial" websites, although their intentions were anything of the sort. I whiled away hours, weeks, days, and then months launching filament, filament, filament out of myself, hoping to connect with another soul, and even resorted to sleeping around in strange hotel rooms with random strangers, and oftentimes asked myself why I had entered into this arrangement. I felt lost and bewildered in this great wide world. All I saw were storm clouds over the horizon: a contentious and consequential Presidential Election was days away, and the days were growing shorter and colder. My nemesis was threatening me with legal action over custody and child support, my parents were growing older, and I too was slowing down perceptibly, having turned fifty a few months ago.

Over the days and weeks that followed, I mellowed somewhat and settled into a spiritual malaise, shunning meaningless associations and nurturing the tight knit group of friends I had acquired over the years. There was an argument to be made for being more insular, more secluded, more cloistered. I rose, or more appropriately shrank, to the occasion, while striving to live a life where I would be surrounded by loving relationships, troops of friends, and an honorable, dignified existence.

Chapter Twenty-Three

The Return of the Prodigal Son

With the realization that I had grown older, with my parents ready to depart and then fade away from the memories of all the people they had known and loved and nurtured, I began to trace the contours of my own life, or what was left of it.

My earliest memories are a collage of emotions and images. I remember pacing back and forth in the corridor of our apartment somewhere in India, eating with relish the mix of boiled potatoes, onions, and spices mom gave to me sometimes. Of dad running after me, trying to teach me how to bike, reading stories to me, and trying in vain to teach me math. So many of those memories are of showering or playing with water in the bathroom. I remember sitting under the tap of our bathroom back in New Delhi when I was just a boy, suddenly getting up, and hitting my head. I think my skull still sports a bump from that mishap! I would just love to splash the walls of the bathroom with water repeatedly and then finally ease into giving a bath to myself.

With barely a year left for retirement and finding myself drifting without ambition or desire, I began to look to Europe or India to spend my remaining time. It would be a welcome reprieve from all associations and the toxic politics of the U.S. Maybe it would cure me of my malaise and restore my spirit.

And yet, as the cliche goes, the more things change.... Around this time, mom began to have vociferous arguments with dad on a regular cadence over my sister. She was the firstborn and so she had held a special place in both parents' hearts for many years. They had coddled her, showered her with every resource imaginable, and consequently she had outperformed at academics and in the game of life, if the object of the game is to accumulate wealth and recognition. Over the years, however, the relationship between mother and daughter had deteriorated, as the weight of slights and hurtful words had steadily accumulated.

"Why doesn't she return my jewelry?" She would often ask in frustration, having given her daughter a fair share during her nuptials.

"Don't ask me, baba," dad would retort. "I never give anything to anyone and then ask for it back."

"Well, it's my property! So what if I gave it to her? I gave it to my daughter, but if my daughter no longer considers me her mother, then she should just return it, especially upon request."

"She says–"

"I know what she says. She says I am not going to take it with me when I die! But so what, neither will she!"

"Ask for it yourself! I don't want to get involved."

"How can I? She no longer talks to me!"

And so it went. The jewelry business metastasized from an open sore to a cancerous canker. Gradually mom derived no satisfaction simply from disowning her daughter; she wanted dad to do the same. "If I were you," she would say to dad, "I would do it in an instant, without hesitation, the way she has disrespected me. It's because you don't support me that this remains unresolved."

As the years went by, they no longer spoke and then no longer spoke well of one another. I wondered if my relationship with my son had deteriorated similarly, but it was a matter of degree. How long had I known my son, after all? How much had I interacted with him? Here, however, there had been a lifetime of effort, from the birthing to the rearing, from the baby's first words and first steps to all the little hurts, sicknesses, trifles and triumphs. A lifetime of experiences and emotional investment. All for naught!

Eventually, after a few pieces of jewelry were returned, rather reluctantly, the atmosphere in the house improved somewhat. It takes tremendous emotional energy to hold a grudge and I suppose it is not easy to maintain that intensity for long.

"Sometimes I feel like a dog," I said to Neal the other day.

"Which breed?" he asked.

"Ha ha! Well, the other day, I was eating Chinese food in the restaurant, and I saw a man bring in his dog, you know, and I am eating my food, and this dog is just going around all over the restaurant, trying to sniff everything and everyone. So he comes around to me and sniffs me as I am trying to slurp up my soup. I think he must have been very hungry or maybe lonely. But anyway –

"Good God, will you get to the point, man?"

"Keep your pants on, Neal, I am getting there. Jeez! So, as I was saying, the man tries to sit the dog down, telling him to sit, pushing down on his rump and so on, but guess what, the dog is in no mood to sit, so he just stands there dumbly, just kind of wagging his tail. Then the man tries to offer him some of his fried noodles, but shit, the dog knows better and doesn't take the bait–

"Hey man, maybe we can continue this convo some other time, huh? I got some errands to run!"

"Will you give me a chance, guy?!"

"Just get to it, will you? It's turning out to be a long *tale*. Get it?"

"Ha ha, yeah I got the pun, my friend! Alright, so basically I am like this dog, just wandering around, sniffing things up and shit, being made to do things, sitting here and there, and not really feeling it, you know. But in the end the dog just gets depressed and crawls under the table and just lays down, you know?"

"And I take it, that's your retirement plan?"

"You know, that's why we are such best buds, Neal. You get me, you really do!"

"So, what do you want to do when you grow up, dude?"

"You mean, when I finally graduate from my job? I don't know, man, I am thinking of hanging it all and just going overseas to maybe like Portugal or Spain."

"Oh yeah? It's not so easy, you know! I mean, do you even speak Spanish or Portuguese? It's hard to get settled in another country, at the tail end of your life, look for lodging, healthcare, and other BS. And you don't even speak the language, for crying out loud. Nope, not that easy!"

"There's that, I suppose, but what the hell am I supposed to do? Hang around in the city, with the frail hope that my son will eventually come to his senses and seek out his father and we will finally be reunited and live happily ever like best friends?"

"Highly unlikely, but yeah, you still don't keep in touch with him?"

"I am cultivating his curiosity, you know? I have changed tactics. I figure, if I don't reach out to him for a few years, maybe he will finally lose whatever toxic sludge has been poured into him and his curiosity will get the better of him. Maybe he will try to seek me out, to understand his roots."

"Maybe. You never know. But is that what you want? I thought you wanted to just hang it all, travel the world, and live the little bit of life you still have left."

"I am conflicted, guy. I know, it's super obvious, right? But what can I do? Depending on the day of the week, I feel differently. Let's see. But I tell you this, for his eleventh birthday I didn't even call him, and such a wave of relief came over me you wouldn't believe Neal."

"Wave of relief? All this time you told me you were dying to see him and hug him and be with him. No?"

"Yeah, I am still his father, and I still feel for him, but not going through the charade of calling him, knowing he has been poisoned against me so much that he wants nothing to do with me, was a relief! I mean, all he wants is to hang up on me as soon as possible, so what's the use? Why go through this circus every time? I even stopped bothering about his healthcare claims and benefit statements in the mail and it's incredible I tell you, making these small but meaningful changes has dramatically improved my mental health!"

"Sure, just neglect him. That's the answer. But whatever man, I am not a dad you know, so I can't claim to understand it."

"No, you can't buddy, but guess what, I feel like I have had just about enough, and sometimes it's just better to walk away from it all. In fact, it's not even that. I feel like in some ways I have disowned him. The limited interaction I have had with him has disappointed me. His lying, shifty eyes on FaceTime, his evasive responses to my questions, his lack of refinement. Shit, that's no son of mine! I know, I know, it sounds horrible and it's unfair to expect so much from a little kid, but like they say, a dream deferred dries up like a raisin in the sun. Heck, after some time my ex even said that he is willing to meet with me briefly and I basically said screw you, just not in those words. Who in their right mind would go all the way over there, almost two hours by bus and train, just to spend an hour or so with the kid? I told her, unless he is willing to spend at least an entire day with me, it's not worth the time and effort to come all the way to see him."

"That seems fair to me. Why should you go for just an hour or two? Have him over for a few hours at least."

"Would you believe, after I told her that, she actually took me up on the offer and said she would drop him off overnight with me and I can drop him back in the evening of the next day."

"Oh really? That's big of her!"

"Ha ha! You would think so, right? But guess what, I refused."

"You did what? You said no?"

"Of course! Think about it Neal! Here's a little kid I know nothing about. He is a stranger to me, and I am a stranger to him. She wants to dump him in my lap, and I have no knowledge of his needs: what medications he takes, allergies he has, chronic conditions, diseases, nothing! And doesn't he need to study? And above all, where will he sleep? Will the whole family be able to sleep peacefully knowing that there is a stranger in the house? God forbid he has one of his asthmatic attacks or something, and then we have to rush to the hospital in the middle of the night. And should he perish, the case can be made that we purposely neglected him, so we won't have to pay child support."

"Geez, Louise! You rocked my world with that one! So many angles to consider."

"Yeah, so, I said tell me all the meds he is taking, all the allergies he has, and then I can bring him home for a few hours for the sibling interaction. But guess what, then she goes off on a tirade about how she needs to see her daughter too and what's my plan for making that happen? So I said, 'fine, you can come to this Starbucks on Queens Blvd., and I will bring the kid, and you can meet her.'"

"And then what?"

"Well, what then? I said I would be there, so I had to go. She ordered a huge coffee drink for Kash laden with sugar and calories, and he slurped it while I talked to him. I noticed as we were chatting how plump he had become and how discolored his teeth were but said nothing."

"Did your daughter talk to her mother?"

"Not really. Maya and Iris sat next to each other and Maya asked her a few questions, but they had nothing to say to each other. I honestly think she is looking to go back to court for child support and visitation again and that's why she is doing all this nonsense. I mean, what other reason could there be? She is looking to show the court that the circumstances have changed, there are regular visits now, and so that should be considered when child support is recalculated."

"I guess, but hey, after all these years you finally met up with your son. How was that experience?"

"That's the funny thing, Neal. So yeah, like I said, I talked to him finally for more than two minutes after almost seven years, and obviously at first we had nothing to talk about, so I started unimaginatively by asking him about his hobbies and interests, and he tells me he likes playing chess, just like me, and enjoys Japanese Anime and Roblox and playing video games. And then, he flips it back to me with my favorite subjects, so I say they are English and History. And then he asks me what I like in History, specifically World History. But not being able to come up with one specific thing, I say, okay, I will give you a few dates and you can tell me why they are important. So I rattle off some dates – 1776, 1492, 1066 and we talk about the American Revolution and Columbus' arrival in the new world etc., and the conversation veers off to the Bubonic Plague in the Middle Ages."

"No! After all this time, you finally meet your son, and you talk about the Bubonic Plague?"

"Yeah, I said the Black Death actually, but he wasn't familiar with that, and kept saying Bubonic Plague, which are one and the same, really. But what's to be done? You know I don't give a rat's ass about the Bubonic Plague and probably he doesn't either, but the lady is sitting there like a hawk, watching our every move, hanging onto every syllable, so that I couldn't really talk freely. But anyway, long story short, we whiled the time away, maybe half an hour or so, just shooting the breeze. After some time, Iris said she was done and wanted to go home, and we called it a visitation."

"What a crock of shit!"

"But wait, it gets better! About a month after this, the lady said to me, 'Kash really needs help with his English homework. Can you help him with that?' Of course, how could I refuse, given my background was in English, so I agreed and suggested that she just drop him off at my house since it will be easier to help him with the homework in person."

"But hold up, didn't you just say there were like a gazillion reasons you *didn't* want to bring him home with you?"

"Yes, there were, there are, and there always will be, but the dad in me took over my brain and I guess I kinda blurted it out before thinking. Anyway, like I was saying, so I take days preparing for his visit, I clean out the cobwebs from my room, make sure the house is spic and span etc., and prepare to welcome him to my house on the appointed day."

"I feel a 'but' coming..."

"Yeah, but not what you think, that he doesn't show up or something. Soon as he gets off the bus stop, he clasps his mother's hand tightly and starts walking towards our house. It's almost like they are lovers or something."

"Oh, I see, so he's a mama's boy?"

"Big time, guy! So he comes, I introduce him to my folks, he sits for like 5 minutes while I serve him a glass of water and a gulp of the smoothie my dad had made earlier in the day, and then he gets up suddenly, complaining of itching around his lips!"

"Wait! What? Are you trying to poison him or something?"

"Ha, ha! Exactly, Neal. You're a quick study, aren't you? You see, the boy is allergic to nuts, all nuts, any kind of nuts, the whole thing is nuts! Dad had put some nuts in that smoothie and they were thoroughly blended in that beverage. Now, I tasted it too, but I couldn't tell, and I didn't remember to tell anyone at home that he was allergic to nuts, so no one could imagine he would have an allergic reaction to it."

"So, he had an allergic reaction? You know, people can die from that kind of stuff."

"Tell me about it. Like 2 minutes after drinking that drink he complains of itchy lips, nausea, and says he wants to throw up, and repeatedly asks for Benadryl. But I don't have any Benadryl, so I rush off to the pharmacy to get some. As I am driving there, this little egg is throwing up in my bathroom (so I was told when I returned home), calling his mom, who in turn is calling me, and acting like he was going to croak any minute now."

"Jeez. That's serious stuff."

"Serious stuff, maybe. I thought it was just so many theatrics and hysterics, it ended up making *me* nauseous! And wouldn't you know it, his mother is just hanging around the neighborhood! Instead of going back home, she comes knocking at my door within half an hour of his arrival. But you know what, I breathed such a sigh of relief after sending him off. This way, I didn't have to drive him all the way back to lower Manhattan, a 36-mile round trip for me, fighting traffic both ways. In such a short amount of time, this little devil made my head spin so fast I saw stars in bright sunlight."

"Now, that's an experience. He came to your home after so many years, only to throw up and run crying back to his mama. My, my! Talk about bad luck!"

"Yeah, I think he inherited his luck from me, and you know

what bad luck I've had in life. But so it goes."

I had hoped to keep the fiction going that I still hadn't seen my son for years. But with Neal it was hard to put up a front. He and I had always talked freely about everything, so why should this be any different? What I *did* manage to keep from him with some effort, though, were my dreams and fantasies about Maya and Kash over multiple years.

Many times, whether sitting quietly somewhere, or dreaming lucid dreams at night, certain thoughts, emotions, and passions would arise in me. I would fantasize about the best way to avenge myself for the lost years, my lost youth, and the irretrievably lost capital. Sometimes I would dream of hiring two strong, burly men, and renting a white van from U-Haul. I would start by waiting outside the State penitentiary and scoping it out for a few days. Then, once I saw the two specimens I thought could do the job, I would send an intermediary over to them to recruit them. Maybe 50k each would suffice? We would have to pick a street corner with as few cameras as possible. Obviously, I would steal the plates off a car parked in a suburban area of the city and screw them on to the van before embarking on our little adventure. I would put on an old hat and grow out my beard and then get behind the wheel. After we kidnap the wench we would drive off to a wooded area somewhere in West Virginia, preferably to an old and deserted log cabin, with hooks in the high ceiling. Through these hooks I would loop a chain, and then denude her and hang her upside down. She would be whipped and forced to divulge the passwords to all her bank accounts and left hanging until the funds transfer into my account was complete. This might take some days, so obviously she would urinate on herself, and maybe some of the spray would come trickling over her belly and boobs, and she would have to turn this way and that just to avoid drinking her own piss. Afterwards, we would bury the body in the woods in an unmarked grave and so get rid of the evidence. Easy peasy!

In another scenario, I wouldn't touch her, but go after the easier target, Kash. Again, these burly guys would kidnap Kash and then

I would drug him into a deep sleep, put him on the back seat of my car, taking care to cover him up completely with a blanket, and I would drive night and day until I got to Mexico. Once there, I could easily sell him or just hand him over to one of the gangs, or put him up for adoption, then come back to New York. After a month or two I would call the wench and ask to speak to him. Obviously, that would be impossible, and so I would petition the court with a writ of habeas corpus and get her in serious legal trouble. That would at least stop all these asinine child support payments.

But these were unnecessary preparations. New York winters were so cold some days that all you had to do was strip someone to their skivvies, chain them to a post or a tree, and leave them there. The cold would do the rest!

Chapter Twenty-Four

A Purposeless Existence

The next time I met Neal he had a dreamy look in his eyes. He had met some lady, as usual, and was all gaga about her. His life was such an emotional roller-coaster, up and down with every hookup and heartbreak. I always wondered why he didn't reflect on what he was doing to himself and take stock of his life, but then I realized he had nothing else to do. He lived alone in his apartment so he was always out and about, frequenting bars, restaurants, cigar lounges, Broadway shows, spitting filament after filament out of himself in the vague hope that it would catch somewhere and ensnare another human being, maybe even a partner for life.

We met for lunch at Fuzi, this up-and-coming pasta place, on a breezy, sunny afternoon. He greeted me enthusiastically and asked about Soni.

"Hey, how is that professor lady of yours these days?"

"She is fine, why?"

"You still seeing her?"

"Well, it's off and on. The last time we spoke it was like 9 p.m. and I was beat. I told her as much, but she wanted to have her convo. So she asks me, 'When are we meeting again?' right, and I dilly dally, like I always do."

"Ha ha! Yeah, you are good at that."

"Oh, to be sure! To be sure. But anyway, I say to her, why don't we just meet as friends, I mean there is value in that. We can go out to eat, see the city etc. Why do we have to go all the way?"

"No way! You said that? Bet she didn't take too kindly to that!"

"100 percent Neal! The lady is like, but no, I like to do more with men."

"Oh yeah, she is just using you for sex."

"I feel like that, you know. I mean, it's a nice problem to have, but sometimes it's too much. Like the other time we met, we go at it once, then a few hours later we do it again, but there is no satisfying this woman. Heck, she wakes up in the middle of the night, or maybe she didn't sleep at all, and it's like 1 a.m. or something and she is moaning and groaning, climbing all over me, saying 'oh baby, baby, let's do it again.'"

"That's some fucked up shit! I had a woman like that once, and I hated it. I get so grouchy when I don't get enough sleep."

"Yeah, me too. But not just that, I actually fall sick. When I came back from seeing her, I had a slight fever, and my head was all stuffed up from a bad cold. I think being naked all night with her lowered my immunity. It was a little cool in the room because she sleeps hot and so I might have caught a cold."

Neal snorted. "Well, it's a good thing you didn't catch anything else, my friend!"

"Ha ha! Nah, man. I took your advice, and I always use a condom. This time I had to because she was on her period. Well, the very beginning of it, actually, so like it wasn't coming out, but if you screwed her your penis would be covered in blood, you know?"

"That's a nice image to hold in your mind! Yeah, I know what you mean."

"Actually, that's the thing that saved me, because I used that to excuse myself from having unprotected sex, you see. She wanted me to ditch the condom and just 'feel me' au natural!"

"That's dangerous. So much can go wrong!"

"Tell me about it! My biggest fear is not even the STDs, but an unintended pregnancy. I mean, it would wipe me out financially, for sure. I might as well commit suicide at that point, you know? I mean, there is no way I can support three kids on my salary."

"You said it!"

Soni was gone. And there were days when I deeply mourned her departure. I took her for granted sometimes, yes, but that was also a coping mechanism of sorts because she wanted me sexually, but I saw her just as a friend; so humor and lightheartedness were the order of the day. And when she left I felt a palpable sense of loss, as if something had been physically snatched away from me. But the hurt was too fresh, and I just couldn't bear to be vulnerable around Neal so soon, so I just pretended the status quo was still in effect.

"How's your dating life going with Krystle?"

"It's coming along. I mean, she is more interested in spending time with her family, you know, than with me."

"You talk to her almost every day, though, right?"

"Yeah, I talk to her, sometimes I see her two or three times per week, but I don't know, man, I get lonely when I don't see her, or she has to spend time with her family."

"It's a different culture. I can understand that though. She is from the Philippines, right? They are very family-oriented over there."

"I guess you are right. But it just seems like our relationship is not a priority for her."

"Sometimes people just want to take their own slow time, you know. Everyone's different."

"Guess so. Hey, how's Uncle Jack doing?"

"Oh God! You had to go and remind me, right Neal? That Jackass! The smallest things are a huge deal with him. Such a micromanager and so superficial. The man disgusts me, so smug and self-serving! Ugh! But you know what, a part of me still admires him. I mean, the guy started out as a volunteer. You know what that means? He rose from nothing to the principalship. Now that's something, isn't it?"

"Yeah, that's something, man. You know what they say, depends on who you know."

"I'll tell you one thing, Neal, as much as I hate his guts, and his foolish utterances, the man is a hard worker."

"Foolishness, like what?"

"Well, for instance, the other day when we were at the training in the city, and my friend Mark and I were sitting next to each other, there was a moment when we had to read and discuss something, and he was like, Mark and Ajay, why don't you guys move closer and work on this. I tried not to react, and neither did Mark, but later we said how ridiculous he sounded. I mean, we are sitting practically cheek to jowl, you know, and this guy is like, move closer! What are we supposed to do? Sit in each other's laps?"

"Ha ha! That's just minor shit, man. Don't you think you are making a big deal out of it?"

"Yeah it's minor but it's the minor annoyances in life that are so, well, annoying! They give you a window in someone else's mind. Show you the composition of their character, you know?"

"Yeah, I hear you. He *is* a bit of a petty bastard."

"Totally petty and small-minded, Neal. Remember, I used to tell you, you can put lipstick on a pig, but it's still a pig! That's what our organization has become. The surface gloss can't always hide the rot inside."

And so the days and weeks and months seemed to drag on. Winters in New York were cold and dark and gray but at least they were peaceful. Summers were noisy and sticky, what with the mechanical whirr of lawn mowers and leaf blowers, the loud mufflers on souped up cars, motorcycles, neighborhood parties and the crackle, pop, and bang of firecrackers around the fourth of July. Sometimes it felt as if one was mechanically going through the motions every day, slowly ambling toward death. A purposeless existence!

Chapter Twenty-Five

Poetry of Departures

As the cliche goes, the world ends not with a bang, but a whimper. There was no grand pronouncement, no doctor with a pale, ashen face, somberly telling me to wrap up my affairs and enjoy my remaining time on earth. No hard to pronounce diseases. It was, instead, a gradual but perceptible diminishment from within. A certain malaise gnawed at me incessantly. It is one thing to wither away physically and another to simply fade away from one's own carefully crafted conception of oneself. When the face that greets you in the mirror each day is less and less familiar, and no longer meets your expectations, then is it really your own?

Besides, sometimes one just gets sick of it all. Sick of all the sanctimony, ceremony, and the requisite unctuousness just to be able to hold down a job that may pay well but punctually rapes your soul each day. And in those dark moments one begins to eye the exits. Surely something more fulfilling, more meaningful and worthwhile hovers just over the horizon? One's existence must mean more! Sartre says that "Hell is other people." But if one cannot avoid hell entirely, there must be some way to at least diminish the intensity of the flames!

So, unsurprisingly, I decided to retire at the earliest opportunity. At sixty-five, the time was neither wrong nor right to change course and escape a dull and dreary existence. I wanted to just flap my wings and perch on new heights, to see what else was out there. And sure enough, when you seek out something new, you usually find it. It may not necessarily be what was sought, but a close enough approximation. For me this meant going back to school and pursuing my passion for the humanities. Fancying myself a fireman, I leapt into the conflagration. When the world was turning away from all that made us human by plunging headlong into artificial intelligence and large language models, when it was embracing technology that could create masterful works of visual art in seconds and write coherently and creatively in an instant, with the consumer culture laser-focused on superfluities and sparklers, I decided to delve into the darkness of the human heart by going back to the basics: reading and writing. I wanted to sit peacefully and savor the flavor and cadence of the written word, to read slowly and ruminate on it, to enmesh myself in the world of ideas. So, naturally, there was little else to do but enroll myself in a doctoral program in English. But having been out of school for decades, I found the process rather daunting. Even getting accepted into a program meant begging the professors for a letter of recommendation.

Things hardly pan out the way one thinks they will. I had made some clear-cut decisions. I had decided to retire and put the past behind me, but the past is always attached to you like a monkey's tail and whatever crud you have dragged yourself in sticks to you all over and especially on your tail, so no matter what, your future self still reeks of your past misdeeds. I was elated when after almost thirty years of graduating from college I was able to apply online to a university and even got accepted. I began preparations for the life of the mind with unbridled enthusiasm and felt invincible. But as I got deeper and deeper into it I was spending long hours on my laptop, in dimly lit rooms, surrounded by books. Sunlight and fresh air seemed a luxury and my eyes ached from staring at computer screens and the printed page. And so just as quickly as I had begun, I abandoned this enterprise and dropped out. I convinced myself this undertaking was going to rob my soul of its remaining sap, mess with my mind and cause premature blindness. I wasn't entirely wrong either. A follow-up visit to the doctor revealed the need for a stronger prescription. Who knows whether it was because of this or just age-related decay or a confluence of factors. And how the heck do you come up with a thesis anyway or even remember what you wrote fifteen pages ago? My memory was beginning to fail me and I was getting more and more agitated and irritable with age.

With no job, and no prospects for one, nor inclination or energy for this sort of thing, the only thing left was to leave the city where I had spent most of my life and start over. Unless you are financially secure, you cannot really retire in New York City. But never mind the urban decay and the high cost of living, the weather was the main consideration. If I cannot really enjoy the great outdoors for five or six months of the year, then what's the point? What keeps a man tethered to a place? If it's not the memories or the opportunity to make a living, it's the people. But bit by bit everything seemed to slowly disintegrate. Meena had taken up permanent residence in Virginia with her darling husband; my son was no longer mine; my parents had passed away; and my only daughter had left the nest.

It wasn't always like this. I remember a time when we didn't have much, but we were close. It was a vibrant time but often suffocating as well. When we were children we fought over the smallest things: a favorite pencil, an unkind word, perceived favoritism by our parents, firecrackers and sparklers saved up for Diwali. It was much harder when we reached adolescence. With the hormones flowing and increased awareness of oneself and others, it was hard sharing a room. The difference in ages, genders, personalities, habits and temperaments made it impossible to stand one another, much less coexist in the same space. Even at night I couldn't rest as I lay in bed, eyes wide open, listening to Meena's snoring.

As the years went on our relationship took further hits. It became more and more apparent that I was always walking on eggshells. Anything I said, or didn't say, would promptly get reported back to dad when he was alive. Sibling rivalry meant discrediting me so thoroughly that there could be no hope of redemption. It was death by a thousand cuts. All these trivialities piled up into a mountain of doubt and disillusionment that colored dad's perception of me. He began to doubt my abilities and intellect, once suggesting that I complete trade school instead of persevering through college because I lacked logical ability. Another time I missed a turn on our way back home from a party and he blew up at me, shouting, "When will you grow up?" I realize now it was likely the regular infusion of poison into his psyche by my toxic sister, rather than anything I had done.

Now I had been left to my own devices and screens, and nothing but. People invariably brought disillusionment, some sooner than others, and so I devoted myself wholly to my art. If I felt like talking to someone I would write in my journal. If I wanted to argue or discuss or bounce ideas off someone I would write dialogue or a short story. The only trouble was I was not good at this stuff. Writing was hard work and often seemed like a waste of time and effort, especially if you ever hoped to get anything published. Almost everyone was a writer but where were all the readers? There were rows and rows of books neatly stacked on library shelves and bookstores and yet all people spoke of when they met was which T.V. show or movie they had recently streamed. Of those who read, how many of them consumed a fast-food diet of romance novels and such paraphernalia? Cafes were full of people sitting and staring at their devices, from phones to tablets to laptop screens. Many of them had their eyes focused on screens and ears covered with headphones, each wholly absorbed in their own world. One left one's house and traded one kind of loneliness for another. Was it better to sit alone and stare at empty walls in an apartment or go to a cafe and be surrounded by a sea of strangers?

Suffocated by a sense of acute people-lessness, my arteries began to stiffen; my eyes, already weakened by age, declined further; and my life force began to ebb. I no longer wanted to go on living such a life. And so I stopped trying. Why bother getting up in the morning, doing my daily ablutions? Why bother with anything, really? I wanted to simply still my mind and body and spirit.

I was never good at goodbyes. In middle school, when it was time to bid farewell to all my friends before boarding the plane to America, I came down with a fever and missed the last couple of days of school. Looking back on it now, it was inconsequential, but it has haunted me since. The transition from high school to college was not much different. I only really had two friends in high school. One guy got a job as a stockbroker on Wall Street and then moved to the Midwest, got married and had kids, (that's what I gleaned from his Facebook profile), and the other lost his dad and financial difficulties compelled him to return to India. Years later, after he and I ran into each other just walking casually down the street, he told me how he had managed to complete his undergraduate degree, then save enough to move to Kansas and go to school there, and finally make his way back to New York City. He went on to get an Electrical Engineering degree from Columbia University and got a job at Citibank. Eventually we lost touch. He got busy with his wife and kids and probably thought it best not to consort with the likes of someone with a mediocre job, no prospects for advancement, and in the middle of a messy divorce. During my years-long divorce proceedings, when I truly needed him most, he went awol.

My ethos in college was to walk the straight and narrow and prove myself to the world. I like to believe I succeeded to some extent in that I didn't end up incarcerated, deported, drugged or dead. I brought no dishonor to my clan or my country. But there is a price for everything, and shunning others at precisely the time when I could have made more of an attempt to be gregarious, now left me friendless and cast aside. I could talk to my AI assistants, but it felt too transactional.

The Dalai Lama has said that all man's troubles come from his inability to sit still. I don't know much about the Dalai Lama, but this rings true for me. All my poor decisions were made in haste or without much forethought. Kismet too played a part, yet all in all it was a full life. All my life I had enjoyed greatly and suffered greatly, both with those that loved me, and alone.

I determined that what little time I had left would be best spent not chasing some holy grail or worldly pleasures but sitting absolutely still. I would sit still and contemplate life, even as cobwebs grew all around me! I would sit in the dark and meditate on the divine light and sound that emanated from within. I would simply sit still; still as I possibly could, so that my essence slowly surfaced and was gradually revealed to me. And as I sat in the deepening dark of the twilight, some lines of verse I had read long ago suddenly came to me:

> I strove with none, for none was worth my strife:
> Nature I loved, and, next to Nature, Art:
> I warm'd both hands before the fire of Life;
> It sinks; and I am ready to depart.

If only it were that simple! Shortly thereafter, bone-tired of sitting perfectly still for a long time, I found myself in the departures terminal at JFK airport. My flight to New Delhi was departing within the hour; my suitcase was checked-in, and air tagged; I was well-equipped with my neck pillow, Kindle, earbuds, eye-mask, large water bottle, and a freshly made fresh mozzarella and tomato sandwich. All that was left to do was to sit back, relax, and enjoy the flight!

Chapter Twenty-Six

The Bitter End

Who knows how long I managed to fight the drowsy numbness that persisted before finally succumbing and passing out during the flight? I felt a hand shaking my left shoulder and a woman's voice calling my name from very far away.

"Mr. Gill, we are deplaning! It is time to disembark, sir."

"Look at that! There, already, huh?" I muttered, groggily.

As I walked through the terminal I dimly recollected how I had packed all my clothes in a huff, sold and donated most of my belongings, and put Neal in charge of selling my house at whatever price seemed reasonable to him. Perhaps trusting Neal with such a consequential task wasn't the wisest course of action, but I had resolved to no longer be a stranger in a strange land. I was born here, and I wanted to die here, among my own folks; the native son returning to a warm embrace of his land and his people.

I mechanically retrieved my luggage from the carousel and plodded along, accompanied by multitudes, jet lagged and disoriented from the journey, but happy to no longer be a pariah. I had yet to leave the airport, but I already felt seen and accepted. In the distance, a man with a black cap and suit was holding up a sign with "Gill" on it. I was under the impression that my cousins were coming to pick me up, but it now seemed they were too busy for these formalities and had sent a car instead.

The driver was fond of Bhangra music, and did his best to make me appreciate it as well. I had to roll up the windows, on account of the dust, heat, and the beggars that mobbed the car with their infant children at almost every stoplight, and that made the music even louder. I was taken by the sights and sounds of this metropolis: cows sitting smack in the middle of the road, unconcernedly chewing their cud in slow, rhythmic motions, and the traffic parting before them like the waters before Moses; dogs sniffing around trash heaps; an occasional monkey or two among the trees, and the sheer number of people on the streets. Times Square seemed like an abandoned village compared to this place. When visitors first alight on this land they often remark how warm and friendly the locals are here, and so this common refrain has not only become a cliche, but a generally accepted euphemism for meddlesomeness. And all too often, people's morbid curiosity in the affairs of others is a direct consequence of a fundamental lack of space and privacy in perhaps the most populous nation on earth.

As I was lost in these reveries, the car suddenly came to a screeching halt. I looked up and saw an imposing mansion. There is no way, I said to myself, that Pankaj and Neeraj have done so well for themselves. They are salaried employees, after all, not businessmen. How could they have built this haveli? Right at that instant the door opened and a tall, lanky man in a kurta pajama, came down the steps. He looked a bit older than me, his prominent nose and scruffy beard taking up most of his visage.

"Namaste," he began. "*Aapki tareef*?"

"Good afternoon," I said. "I am Ajay Gill. And you are?"

"I am Mukesh. I don't believe we have met. You were picked up at the airport?"

"Yes, of course. The driver had a placard with my name and I just followed him and got in the cab."

"Unbelievable! He's done it again!" he fumed. "Surya, come here!" He beckoned the driver and spoke to him menacingly in low tones."

"I am sorry, Mr. Gill," he said. "There seems to have been some misunderstanding. Our driver is new, and he doesn't know the family as well as he should. Be that as it may, he should have at least verified your identity before bringing you all the way here. He will immediately take you back to the airport now. I am very sorry for the inconvenience, but please understand that I was expecting my nephew with the same surname as yours, and he must still be at the airport, poor boy, wondering why no one came to receive him."

"Oh my! I see. But it's no trouble at all. I can manage, if you can just direct me to—"

"Please accept our apologies, sir. Surya will take you back promptly," he said, as he practically shoved me back in the car and slammed the door on me. Surya, embarrassed and humiliated, apologized profusely and we instantly commenced our journey back to the airport.

The traffic was at a standstill, and Surya started taking shortcuts through narrow alleys and backstreets, incessantly honking his horn and speeding dangerously, to clear away the kids playing in the middle of the street. Being in transit at such length activated an array of symptoms in my being, from the mildly irritating borborygmus to vertigo and an urge to vomit. I had no one to blame but myself. If I had only stuck up a conversation with the asinine driver, this could have been easily avoided; but no, I had to be my antisocial self. The loud, Punjabi music was the real villain though.

"Hai Ram!" uttered Surya and pulled over to the side just as we were making our way through a rubble-strewn road.

"Dear God! What now?" I asked and got out of the car to look. The left rear tire had gone flat, and the vehicle was tilted to one side. I became increasingly overwhelmed by the constant noise of the traffic, the incessant honking from all sides, the oppressive heat, even though it was nearly dusk, and the streetlights had begun to come on, and the pervasive smell of smoke in the air.

"What is all that smoke?" I asked.

"That is the pollution, sir!" he replied. "The farmers in Punjab clear their fields this time of year, *sirji*, and the smoke from the fires drifts down to us."

The main terminal of the airport rose prominently in the distance. I thanked Surya, retrieved my suitcase and started making my way there. It was getting dark now and I quickened my pace, somewhat apprehensive about losing my way in a new city. I simply couldn't bear to sit anymore, and despite the noise, smoke, heat, and now the little insects that kept nipping away at my arms and buzzing around my ears, I thought it best to just foot it, rather than wait for Surya to change the tire and thus waste more time. Besides, growing fatigue and the urge to empty my bowels made the decision even easier.

In the crush of humanity that is New Delhi, the assailants stole right behind me unnoticed and clobbered me on the right side of my head. I staggered forward, then fell back and hit the ground. In the encroaching dusk, as I lay on the dusty road, half-conscious and overcome with thirst, something warm and sticky ran down my face. I tried to lift myself but collapsed instantly, my head throbbing. My senses were saturated with all the sights and sounds–the blare of traffic, the yellow glow and hiss of gas lamps, the heat waves rising into the thick air, and throngs of people everywhere.

When I came to, I found myself in a small, dark, and poorly furnished room. Some good Samaritan must have taken pity on me and brought me to his home, I thought. But by and by, a sinister realization seeped into me. I was penniless! I had lost my passport, identification, and luggage. Who could help me? What was this place where I now found myself, a stranger among my own people? I had intended on visiting my cousins, Pankaj and Neeraj, but I had no way to contact them now.

As I deliberated what to do, a compartment in the lower half of the door to the room slid open and a metal plate came swooshing toward me. It held a small bowl with what looked like dal, and two dried up rotis.

"Eat!" a voice commanded and instantly shut the compartment in the door.

Eating was the furthest thing from my mind. I banged on the iron door, shouted at the top of my lungs, threatened, begged, pleaded, but to no avail. Days went by, then weeks, then perhaps months, with no human contact. I would use the toilet attached to the room, eat my meager meals in silence, and sit propped up against the wall all day, too morose to move. This sedentary lifestyle gradually robbed me of the ability to think clearly, as cobwebs built up in my mind, my joints ached more than ever, and I started to question reality itself. I inspected every nook and crevice in the room to find an opening but found it challenging with the concrete floors and impregnable walls. Curiously enough, there were no sounds from the outside world: nothing but silence.

I tried reasoning with my captors. "I am an American," I declared loudly. "With money!" I clarified. "Just let me go. I will make it worth your while if you release me!"

After several months (I had stopped tallying my days on the walls a long time ago), the door opened, and my heart played hopscotch. Two masked, burly men, dressed all in black, approached with lathis and started beating me mercilessly. After they had broken every bone in my body, they took out a piece of paper and a pen and motioned to me to sign the document. I could barely read, what with tears streaming down my cheeks and hands that shook violently, but I signed anyway just to get rid of them.

Sometimes, late at night, I would hear the disembodied voices of these two men, conspiring together in low tones. I think I once made out the words, *"paisa,"* *"buddha,"* and "social," and a sigh escaped my lips. With the dawn of each day I journeyed westward and felt myself slipping away. Any physical activity exhausted me. Even moving from one corner of the room to another seemed like a big production and utterly pointless.

What was left now but old memories? When one retreats from the senses one invariably notices the indentations and recesses of one's own mind. I recalled my life in New York City, particularly the nights spent frequenting The Bitter End on Bleecker Street in the heady days of my youth to listen to cover bands, hang out with strangers, and soak in the atmosphere. I wouldn't leave until almost closing time, after spending the day playing chess at Washington Square Park with the hustlers, eating the most delicious ramen ever, and catching a movie in the theatre. Once, late at night, as I was making my way back to the subway, I chanced upon a homeless man, squatting in the corner with his pants down. He gave me a look of fear and reproach but proceeded nevertheless with his business. It was this grittiness that gave New York its character. This in-your-face no-holds-barred attitude that repulsed so many but endeared others to its metropolitan charms.

By and by a slow change came over me. Sitting motionless for days on end stiffened my joints, stilled my spirit, and clouded my brain. Occasionally, my captors would enter and survey the room, but now even with them I had no human interaction other than signing a few papers every now and then. During these years of uninterrupted solitude ideas and sensations flowed into me and then just as easily flowed out. And while it was physically debilitating to lose much of my sight and hearing, it was liberating to expunge my mind of all anger, hatred, envy, vindictiveness, and pettiness. A profound feeling of acceptance and transcendence had swelled up in me and I embraced it with all my being.

Bibliography

Arnold, Matthew, "Dover Beach"

Auden, W. H., "As I Walked Out One Evening" & "Musée Des Beaux Arts"

Baldwin, James, "Sonny's Blues"

Dickinson, Emily, "After great pain, a formal feeling comes –" & "Tell All the Truth But Tell it Slant"

Eliot, T.S., "The Love Song of J. Alfred Prufrock" & "The Waste Land"

Forster, E.M., A *Passage to India*

Hemingway, Ernest, *To Have and Have Not* & *The Sun Also Rises*

Landor, Walter Savage, "Dying Speech of an Old Philosopher"

Larkin, Philip, "Poetry Of Departures"

Levertov, Denise, "The Ache of Marriage"

Lord Tennyson, Alfred, "Ulysees"

Mathers, Shannon. (Director). (2011). *A Very Short Engagement* [Film; Final cut]. University of Southern California, School of Cinematic Arts

McCullers, Carson, *The Heart Is a Lonely Hunter*

Nietzsche, Friedrich, *Beyond Good and Evil: Prelude to a Philosophy of the Future*

Shakespeare, William, *Macbeth*

Smith, Stevie, "Not Waving, But Drowning"

Turgenev, Ivan, *Fathers and Sons*

Whitman, Walt, "A Noiseless Patient Spider"